IT'S A HIT!

By Arin Cole Barth
and Marika Barth

First edition, 2022

 But remember, you have the right to be safe, strong, free, and utterly fabulous in whatever gender(s) you choose. Don't let anyone tell you otherwise. This is a secret message from a happy, well-loved adult trans person. You're wonderful, and there are plenty of people in the world who will love you just as you are.

Book Design: kd diamond
Cover art: Holly McGillis

ISBN: 978-1-9991562-9-9

Published by Flamingo Rampant

www.flamingorampant.com

10 9 8 7 6 5 4 3 2 1

Printed in Korea

For my father, David, and my brother, Rio, who were my first models of healthy masculinity. Thank you for showing me how varied and wonderful it can be. And for my mother, Hadley, who will always be my confidante and the first person I turn to for advice. Thank you for listening and caring, no matter how our experiences differ.

- Marika

To all the young queer and trans kids learning about and growing into their identities. I'm so proud of you. You're doing wonderfully, and it's okay if you don't have everything figured out yet. It may be hard to believe sometimes, but there will always be someone in your corner.

- Arin

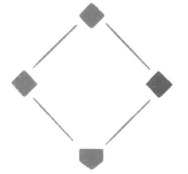

Part One

Taylor

"So, the top is the first part. And, the bottom is the last part. Is there a middle part?" his Nanay asked, glancing into the rearview mirror. Their attention was split between the road and the conversation. Their brows furrowed, as they tried to parse out the mysteries of baseball.

Taylor appreciated it. He really did. His moms were the best. They came to all of his games. Prodded everyone in their family to buy chocolate bars during fundraising season. Were the first to sign up for the snack roster. They supported him. And that was great.

But, goodness, the two of them would never understand baseball. His Ma had given up early. Giving him a hug and a kiss and saying "oh well." Right now she was buried in a book, not paying the slightest bit of attention to the conversation. But his Nanay kept trying. And, honestly, there were only so many times he could try to explain it to them.

"The middle part is when the two teams switch positions." He clarified, trying hard to keep the exasperation out of his voice. "I know, Nanay. It's okay. I don't expect you to get baseball." Taylor continued, aiming for reassurance, not entirely certain whether he was managing it.

"I know, kiddo." They smiled, and he was thankful they both

were in the car. He knew that look. His Nanay would be ruffling his hair if they could. It wasn't that he minded it exactly, but it made him feel younger than he was. "But, it's important to you," they said. "We certainly subject you to enough of our interests. I want to understand yours as well."

Taylor couldn't argue with that. He'd grown up going to drag shows and pride parades and demonstrations and comic cons and Dungeons & Dragons sessions. His first drag show he'd been all of five weeks old, and his Ma had been performing. He'd also been used as a prop in D&D more than once as a small child.

Some of his friends seemed to have a hard time imagining their parents doing anything outside of them. But that wasn't his moms. When he came along, they'd stayed involved in everything they already did, just with him in tow.

Maybe it was because they were so young when they had him. Maybe it was because they had such a large collection of chosen family to spoil and babysit him. Maybe it was just because they were too giant of nerds to stop.

Regardless, he had a giant collection of knowledge about D&D and drag and all things nerdy that he was never going to need. But that was fine. It didn't mean that his Nanay needed to understand baseball in return. He didn't have the words to tell them that though, so he continued the discussion, filling in bits and pieces in response to their questions, settling in to enjoy the drive.

It was relaxing enough. His baseball trivia was every bit as automatic as his knowledge of Star Trek or Glam Rock, if a bit more relevant to his actual interests. It was easy to provide answers without having to pay too much attention. And no one could say that the Rocky Mountains didn't provide a gorgeous view.

Wil

"There's the National League and the American League. They mostly play by the same rules, but in the AL each team has a designated hitter who only bats and isn't a position player," his dad explained with an air of expertise, tinged with excitement. "It said on the website that your camp is using a designated hitter."

Wil didn't entirely know what it meant to be a "position player," but he was certain he'd learn soon enough. He probably ought to pay more attention now. Especially because it was apparently relevant to how Young Sluggers Baseball Camp, his camp for the summer, was set up.

Sports had never really been his thing, and baseball seemed particularly complicated. With all the rounds and numbers and different positions, it was hard to follow, and when he tried, he just found himself getting stressed out.

The closer they got, the more he regretted ever agreeing to this. He just knew it was going to be a disaster. He'd never been good at sports. The rules didn't make sense, and his hand-eye coordination was pathetic.

He was bound to be the laughingstock of the whole camp. A nerdy, little, trans boy who couldn't even throw a ball straight much less keep up with the rules of the game. His dad had been so excited, talking about how much he'd loved baseball camp as a kid and what a great experience it would be for him.

He'd been trying so hard ever since Wil came out, wanting to support him. He just... kind of didn't have any clue how. Wil hadn't had the heart to explain that just because he was a boy, he didn't suddenly like baseball. It was boring and complicated, and he'd much rather be imagining fantasy worlds with his friends.

So, now instead of heading back to his nice, friendly theater camp that he'd attended every summer since he was six, he was currently on his way to baseball camp. Of all places. What had he gotten himself into?

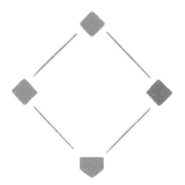

Taylor

By the time they pulled into the parking lot, Taylor was already grinning wide. This was his place where he was in his element. He loved his family to death, but none of them really got this side of him.

"It's just the same," he exclaimed excitedly, looking out the windows. Other campers were already beginning to unload, but they were still too far away for him to tell if he recognized anyone.

"Well, not just the same," his Nanay observed. "You know all that work your Ma did to convince them to add gender-affirming rooming options finally paid off."

"Yeah. That's great, Ma. Good for you."

"Aww. Thanks, honey." She barely looked up from her book, but her response was still genuine.

"Some of your friends were coming back this year, weren't they?" His Nanay asked, looking around for an open parking spot.

"Yeah. Mateo and Jessie and a few others I don't know as well," Taylor replied distractedly, peering out the window to see if he could spot anyone familiar.

"But you don't mind not rooming with any of them?" they checked in. He should have known that's where this conversation was going. Nanay always worried about pushing things onto him. "You know you didn't have to mark that you were good with a gender-inclusive room."

"Nah," he replied casually. "It's not a problem. Mateo and Jessie are rooming together this year, now that they can. And I'm not as close to any of the others. Besides, I like meeting new people."

Taylor shrugged, but he meant it. If he'd wanted to room with one of his friends, he would have requested it.

He was excited there were more gender-affirming options now, honestly. And he definitely didn't want some poor kid who'd requested a gender-inclusive room to not get one because no one else had marked that they were okay with it.

"Okay, kiddo. I know you'll always tell me what you need. I just like to check in." His Nanay didn't press, their focus shifting towards maneuvering the large car into the parking spot they had finally found.

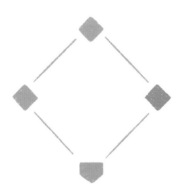

Wil

Wil looked around the area as they wove through the lot looking for a parking space. Wow. There were certainly a lot of boys here. Maybe forty or fifty in various stages of unloading and checking in.

There were a couple who looked nervous and hesitant, but most of them were obviously excited. Pointing out different things to the adults dropping them off. They all looked like they had a lot more equipment than he did. Wil saw bags stuffed with bats and gloves and even helmets. A lot of the boys were wearing baseball caps or shirts Wil vaguely recognized as being for the Colorado Rockies, the team his dad liked. Other kids wore different colors and logos. Probably for other teams that Wil didn't recognize.

"This is an all-gender camp, right?" he confirmed, looking around a bit warily. Not that he didn't like guys or anything. Heck, he was one. Still, he didn't always feel super comfortable around just boys. He'd never actually been in an all-boys environment before, and he wasn't certain how to feel about it.

"Yeah. I even called and double-checked." His Dad confirmed, clearly sensing his worry. "They've got that gender-affirming rooming thing and everything." He continued, handling the words "gender-affirming" a bit gingerly, as if they didn't sit quite right on his tongue.

"You'll be just fine, sport. I promise you're going to love it here." A promise Wil had heard a lot over the past couple of weeks, as his Dad clued into his growing uneasiness. He didn't quite trust it. But he knew his dad meant well. He could survive anything for three weeks. Couldn't he?

"Hey. You never know. Maybe your roommate will be transgender too?" His dad proposed with forced light-heartedness. Looking uncertain and a bit uncomfortable all of a sudden, he shifted his grip on the steering wheel restlessly.

"Yeah. Maybe." Wil mumbled, knowing that wasn't going to help his dad any, but unable to muster the energy to be optimistic. Really, what were the chances of that? How many other trans kids decided to attend baseball camp, of all things?

He stared resolutely out into the parking lot, feeling more discontent by the second, when they passed a large car parked on their left. He wouldn't have noticed it, except the back was completely plastered with bumper stickers, half bad puns and half in support of almost every major social justice issue he'd heard about and some he hadn't.

Even with the car driving slowly, navigating a parking lot full of campers, he didn't have time to read them all. But one caught his eye. Printed with the trans flag as a background, it read "I left my gender in my other car." Kind of a pathetic joke, but he chuckled at it anyway. He felt a glimmer of hope in his chest. Maybe there were other trans kids here.

Maybe this would be all right after all.

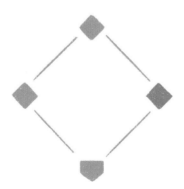

Taylor

"Thanks, Nanay. Thank you, Ma. I love you both." Taylor smiled and laughed. He'd been trying to shoo them away for the past ten minutes, but he knew they wouldn't be going anywhere for at least another ten, and he didn't really mind. He also knew that if he actually asked them to leave, they'd respect it and go.

"We're going to miss you, kiddo." His Ma hugged him again. She'd even put her book away to help him unpack. A rarity when she was that close to the end of a story. He could already predict that Nanay would have a quiet car ride home.

"I'm gonna miss you too, Ma." He squeezed tight, letting himself lean against her tall frame. "I love you so much." Every year he fought back tears when they dropped him off. Excited as he was, he'd always been a crier. He got it from her.

Sure enough, his Ma was blinking away tears as well. "Love you too, pumpkin." She kissed the top of his head before releasing him, letting his Nanay wrap him up instead in one of their tight short hugs that ended with them pulling away and ruffling his hair. Taylor resisted the urge to duck away, hating how much less comfortable that had gotten over the past year.

"Have a great time, hon," his Nanay finished, not noticing his slight discomfort. And, with that, they took his Ma's hand and the two of them were off, shouting approximately a dozen "goodbyes" and "we love yous!" over their shoulders as they left.

Taylor brushed the tears from his eyes, turning to look over his space. His moms had helped him get everything set up before they left, so now he was on his own. Free to chill until the rest of the campers arrived. He was debating pulling out a graphic novel versus just hanging out and listening to his baseball music playlist when the door swung open again.

"Oh, sorry, didn't realize anyone else was here." The new kid muttered awkwardly, juggling too many bags in their short arms.

"Here. Let me help you with those," Taylor said, rushing forward, relieving the kid of a couple of the more precariously held items and setting them down on one of the dressers. "And, no worries. This is your room too. At least, I assume it is?" He plopped back down on his own bed.

"Uh. Yeah? Room 216." The kid still seemed uncomfortable, setting down their own bags and resolutely avoiding eye contact. Not that eye contact was a must or anything. Taylor wasn't fond of it himself, though he could fake it if he had to. But this kid seemed more like someone who was totally freaked out than someone who just didn't enjoy eye contact.

"Yeah. You're in the right place then. I'm Taylor. He/him pronouns." He rolled back to his feet and stuck out a hand.

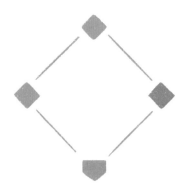

Wil

Wil hadn't expected his roommate to be so big. Or so cute.

The boy standing across from him was tall and heavyset, with curly brown hair and equally dark eyes. Wil couldn't help but notice that he had just one dimple when he smiled. On the left. It made him look adorably lopsided.

And, now he was way too distracted. This guy was big. Practically twice his size. He probably loved sports. He was going to eat Wil for breakfast.

Or help him with his bags? Apparently, that was what was happening. Which was distracting also, because as it turned out he was pretty muscly. This was really not what Wil needed to be thinking about now.

Steadfastly ignoring looking at his new roommate, Wil focused on setting down the rest of his luggage. He'd convinced his dad to leave right after check-in, where he had already asked about a million questions, suddenly really worried about Wil. His dad's overprotectiveness could be a lot, and he appreciated being left alone, so he could relax and not be constantly reassuring him. But that also left him to drag all his stuff to the room by himself.

It was only when the other boy stood back up and stepped closer, introducing himself, that Wil let himself look again. He was cute. For all that he was absolutely massive, he didn't look mean. He honestly seemed like a nice guy. Wil could do this. He could do this.

Wait? Pronouns. He backtracked, replaying the conversation in his head. Yeah. His roommate, Taylor, had introduced himself with pronouns.

He looked closer. Taylor didn't look trans. Then again, that was just a stereotype. There's no one way trans people look.

It's not like Wil really knew any other trans folks in person. He couldn't just go off what he saw on Tumblr and on those weird documentaries his dad kept streaming where they misgendered the people through the whole thing.

"I'm Wil. He/him also," he finally managed after what felt like an awkwardly long pause. "It's good to meet you. I guess we're rooming together?" He could kick himself. It was such a stupid question. Obviously, they were rooming together. Taylor was already unpacked.

Taylor. His roommate. A cute boy. Who'd introduced himself with his pronouns? And who was big enough to protect him, maybe, if there was any kind of trouble.

Wil found himself thinking again that maybe this summer wouldn't be that bad.

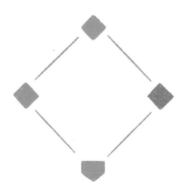

Taylor

Wil seemed... kind of squirrely. But Taylor didn't hold it against him. His Nanay and half of his family had social anxiety too. He was used to it.

Besides, it was pretty common for people to be thrown when he introduced himself with pronouns. Most cis people still weren't used to it. At first, he'd thought Wil was trans, but who really knew? His Ma was always talking about how you can't tell someone's trans status just by looking at them.

Not that she bothered to hide her own. He chuckled to himself. About half of her t-shirts said something about being trans (the other half were ridiculously nerdy).

"Good to meet you too." He smiled, trying to put the other boy more at ease. "I like your name. Cool spelling." He nodded at Wil's nametag, strung loosely about his neck.

"Oh. Thanks. I like it. It's after Wil Wheaton. I, um, I really look up to him. He's a cool guy and everything. And he played Wesley Crusher, one of my favorite characters. I always wanted to be him when I grew up. And then, Wil Wheaton himself is actually a really good person too, like, in real life. And..." He trailed off, looking uncomfortable as if he'd only just realized that he'd started rambling.

"Yeah. Wheaton seems cool. I've gotta admit Wesley isn't my favorite though," Taylor replied, trying to put Wil at ease. He still seemed so on edge, Taylor just wanted to let him know everything was okay.

"You like Star Trek?" Wil asked, seeming cautious.

"I think it's all right. Not my go-to, but my Ma loves it so I've watched plenty. She's more of a TOS fan to be honest, though."

"Seriously? That's my least favorite series. But fair enough." Wil replied, much more naturally. Taylor got the impression that once you got him started talking about Star Trek, he'd be hard to stop.

"What's your favorite?" Taylor asked because he'd never minded listening to someone geek out about something they loved. And with that he was able to settle back on his bed and simply listen to Wil talk excitedly while he unpacked.

Wil

"A bunch of people hate the Enterprise theme song, and I've never really understood why. Sure, it's different, but..." Wil caught sight of Taylor again and trailed off. He was sprawled out across his bed, fidgeting with some small, metal thing. His eyes were on the top bunk, not following Wil at all.

"I'm sorry. Was I boring you?" Wil asked, feeling shy and embarrassed again. The first person he met at baseball camp, and he revealed himself to be a giant nerd. Of course, no one here was going to want to hear him talk about Star Trek endlessly. He mentally kicked himself.

"What?" Taylor sat up suddenly and hit his head on the top bunk. "Ow!" he exclaimed, rubbing the bump. "These beds get shorter each year, I swear." He chuckled, seeming to conclude he wasn't too terribly hurt.

"You weren't boring me." Taylor continued. "I like hearing people talk about things they're passionate about. Sorry if I didn't seem like I was paying attention. I was listening. I just don't always remember to track people and stuff." He shrugged as if that was a normal comment.

"Oh. Okay. Well, just say if I ever do start boring you? I know you probably don't care about nerdy stuff like that. Star Trek's really just for geeks, isn't it?" He found himself saying with a shrug. He'd learned what he needed to do to fit in a long time ago, dismissing his interests, hiding. Of course, the rules were different now. Expectations for boys were so different than those for girls. But this had probably stayed the same, right?

"Not if you're gonna say it like that." Taylor looked up again, almost making eye contact. "Sure it's for geeks. But geeks are awesome!" He spoke with genuine excitement. "Everyone's a geek about something, right? The world would be boring if we weren't."

Wil was kind of taken aback. Taylor seemed... passionate about this. Genuinely concerned that Wil had been dismissive of his own interests, but also just passionate in general. About what? People being geeks? It was weird. Not something he'd ever encountered from any of the kids back home.

By then, Wil was just about finished unpacking. He hesitated before pulling out the posters he normally brought to theater camp every year. Taylor seemed nice enough, but Wil was still nervous that he'd get made fun of if he hung them up. The dorm room was pretty sparse, with bunk beds and a couple of desks, but Taylor hadn't done much to decorate. There was a photo on his desk but nothing else. So maybe decorations were less the norm here?

Wil left the posters tucked away and stowed his suitcase under the bed, feeling a little sad about it. The room sure could use some decoration. It had dull white walls that reminded WIl of every motel room he'd stayed in, and one small window that looked out on a brown courtyard. *I'll hang them up later*, he promised himself, not entirely sure he believed it.

Straightening up, Wil caught a glance of Taylor still sprawled out on the bed. He couldn't stop noticing his cute hair and arms. Taylor caught him looking and smiled at him. Wil fought back a blush. If he kept up like this, Wil was at risk of developing a serious crush. But maybe they could at least become friends?

Taylor

The first meal at camp was always dinner. The camp had reserved a section of square tables at the dining hall just for their group. A bunch of them were always pushed together to make one long table, but a few were left on their own, including Taylor's favorite.

Their floor leader, a guy named Colin who'd worked for the camp for a few years, walked their floor group over. Taylor decided to stay close to Wil on the way there, so he wouldn't be alone. The poor guy still seemed super uncomfortable.

They were the first group to make it to the dining hall, which meant they had first pick of the tables. "Come on," he said to Wil before heading directly to his favorite table in the corner. "This is the best table."

"It is?" said Wil, seeming to calm down enough to talk more naturally as everyone dispersed among the various tables. Taylor was glad that he seemed more comfortable now, at least.

"Absolutely. It's the quietest and the sound only comes from one direction, instead of all around you. And from this seat—" he sat down, "you can see everyone coming into the dining hall." Taylor explained with an easy smile.
Wil was still standing nervously next to the table. "Here," Taylor said, "take this seat next to me. Jessie and Mateo will want to sit next to each other anyway."

"Who?"

"My friends. They're—" Taylor spotted them walking inside with their floor group, "They're right there, look." Wil looked at the new group, still pretty quiet. He was probably overwhelmed with all the new people. Taylor knew the feeling.

He half stood out of his chair and waved until Jessie and Mateo spotted him. They picked up the pace, weaving in and out of the narrow paths through the dining hall, racing to the table where Wil and Taylor were waiting. Jessie elbowed past Mateo as they picked up speed, and he tripped slightly on one of the table legs. "Walk, please," Colin called out. They giggled and slowed down.

Taylor rolled his eyes from where he was watching. Jessie and Mateo were always like this. Mateo squeezed past Jessie on his way into the seat across from Taylor. "I beat ya, ha!" he said, and Jessie made a face as she sat next to him. "Who's this?" she asked. "I don't recognize you."

"This is my roommate, Wil," Taylor said. He really wanted to introduce Wil properly, to tell his best friends here all about what a nerd he was and how much he loved Star Trek, but he didn't know how much Wil would be comfortable with him sharing, so he left it at that. Wil could decide what he wanted them to know and when.

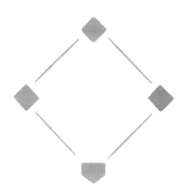

Wil

Wil sat frozen in his seat as two jock-looking kids came barreling toward them. A boy with dark, wavy hair tripped slightly, laughing and revealing his crooked teeth as he did. A slightly taller girl with long braids tied into a high ponytail got ahead of him, grinning widely herself. Wil felt like he wanted to run. Or better yet, disappear. He'd already had to interact with one new human today, and while dinner was inevitable, he was kind of hoping to avoid too many more the first night.

Not that he didn't want to meet people. He was just worried they wouldn't want to meet him, especially when they realized he didn't know anything about the game they were here to play. Literally, the entire point of this camp was baseball. He was going to stick out like Elphaba at Shiz University.

"Wil, this is Mateo, he/him pronouns," Taylor got his attention, indicating the boy sitting in front of him, "and Jessie, she/her," he pointed at the girl.

Jessie sat up straight in her seat and held out her hand across the table. Wil took it cautiously, and she shook it once. "Good to meet you, Wil. What do you play?"

"Uhhh…" Wil's first thought was a tiefling ranger but somehow he didn't think that was what she was going for. This camp was about baseball not Dungeons & Dragons. "I, uh, haven't played much."

"Ahh, okay. Well, I'm usually second base and Mateo here tries to pass himself off as an outfielder when they don't let him be the DH."

"Hey, at least I can hit the ball more than ten feet," Mateo shot back.

"At least I can throw," Jessie retorted. Mateo stuck his tongue out in response.

Wil watched this whole interaction silently, trying to keep up and very quickly getting bogged down by questions he didn't want to ask. Outfielder? DH? At least he thought he knew what second base was. Luckily, he was spared having to respond when an older woman with greying dreadlocks climbed up on a chair in the middle of the dining area, and called out, "Okay, attention! Your attention, please!

"Welcome everyone, to the fifteenth annual Young Sluggers Baseball Camp!" At this point, all the kids started clapping and a few gave loud whoops of excitement. "Okay, settle down. Quiet, please. As some of you may know, I'm your camp director and head coach, Coach Rose. I'm excited to kick things off! First, some reminders. We are guests in this space. It is all of our responsibility to keep it clean and take care of it. Clear away your dirty dishes, clean up your spills, push in your chairs, et cetera.

"Second, this evening is for settling in. Talk to new people, start getting to know each other. The people sitting around you will be your teammates during this camp, and you may be playing with them for our weekend games. But those rosters won't be released until a few days from now, and you will practice with kids from other teams, so even then, everyone is on everyone's side. Help each other. Learn together.

"Dinner will end at 7:30. After that, we'll head back to the dorms for a fun surprise and icebreaker games in your floor groups. Now go get your food!"

Mateo and Jessie raced back out of their seats, headed in the direction of the pizza station. Wil started to get up too but stopped when Taylor stayed put. "You okay?"

"Oh, yeah. Fine," he said. "I'm just going to wait until everything has settled down a bit. You go ahead." He waved Wil off nonchalantly.

"Okay," Wil said. He'd seen some chicken nuggets on the way in and his stomach was rumbling. He had the feeling by now that Taylor didn't plan on leaving him alone.

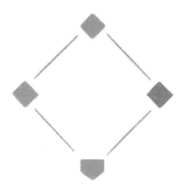

Taylor

Taylor was glad to see that Wil seemed to get on all right with Jessie and Mateo. Wil had looked overwhelmed at first, but once he'd had a chance to acclimate to their constant teasing, he'd seemed to relax. Taylor himself was really happy to see them. It sucked that they all lived so far away from one another.

He let himself settle back and enjoy dinner, watching as Jessie competently facilitated the discussion. "What's your social media?" was one of the first questions she demanded of Wil.

"I bet he has TikTok. You look like the kind of guy who would have TikTok," Mateo tossed in with an analytical expression. Jesse looked at him and nodded in agreement.

Taylor still wasn't entirely certain what TikTok was or how it worked. He knew it involved videos if that got him any points. Jessie liked to regularly remind him that she'd had to set up his Snapchat for him and teach him how to use it.

But, Wil apparently wasn't the technological inept Taylor was and seemed happy to exchange codes or handles or whatever they were. It was nice. Taylor wasn't really worried that they wouldn't get on. After all, cool people generally did. But, still, there was a part of him that really loved seeing everyone he liked making friends with one another.

"Taylor here is still practically a grandpa," Jessie observed, right on cue. Taylor sent her a halfhearted glare, more for show than anything else. "I do have Snapchat," he protested, sharing his own handle.

"Yeah. But nothing else." Mateo remarked with a good-natured laugh. "And, you barely know how to use it." Jessie chipped in. Taylor chuckled as well. "True. I don't know how you all keep up with that stuff. I swear there are different expectations for every single app."

It was overwhelming, for all that everyone else seemed into it. "That's half the fun!" Jessie remarked with a grin, and Taylor noticed Wil nodding along. "Cool. Y'all have fun then. Snap away."

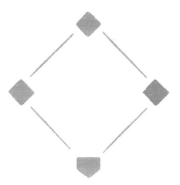

Wil

Wil felt a lot more at ease by the time they got back to their dorm. The "welcome back to camp" show the counselors put on was pretty ridiculous. And actually kind of... sweet? Especially, considering that he'd expected it all to be Hoo-Rah He-Man stuff. The icebreaker games were pretty standard and also so cheesy. How many times had Wil come up with an animal that started with the first letter of his name before? He was definitely a woodpecker. He knew that about himself.

He figured there were some things that were true of any camp. The sense of home that returners felt was probably one of them.

"Six texts, really?" he remarked, looking up from his phone in surprise. He'd kept it in his pocket during the show, not wanting to be completely rude. But apparently, his dad had been even more freaked out than Wil had realized.

There was a long string of one concerned text after another. "Hey, I probably ought to call my dad back," he told Taylor, stepping into the hallway and looking for somewhere quiet. His dad was perfectly capable of texting but definitely preferred phone calls. He liked to say he was "old school."

"Dad, how's it going?" Wil aimed for a cheery tone, not having to try that hard to get there. He'd actually had a fun evening. "Worried much?" he remarked with a laugh. Gee, he wondered where he got his anxiety from.

His dad acknowledged it easily enough, already seeming to feel better now that he had finally got ahold of Wil. "Don't be, really," Wil tried to reassure him. "Honestly. I like my roommate and I met a couple of his friends. Everyone seems pretty all right so far." Sure, he didn't know how the actual baseball-ing would go, but at least he was getting along with people.

His dad seemed relieved at that. Wil could tell that his own anxieties had gotten to him. Any time Wil was really worried about something, his dad started to fret as well. And vice-versa, to be honest. It was a stellar combination, really.

But thus far, the camp wasn't turning out to be quite as terrifying as Wil had feared. Sure, everyone was sporty, but Jessie hadn't held it against Wil when he made it clear that he wasn't. And it wasn't like sports was the only thing anyone talked about here. Just that night Jessie and Mateo had a rousing debate about sledding versus snowball fights.

Wil didn't stay on the phone much longer after finally calming his dad down some. He never really knew what to talk about when his dad just wanted to chat. But after he hung up, he stayed out in the little lounge he'd found, messaging his friends from home.

Leila was going to want to hear all about Taylor. And yeah, Wil wouldn't mind spending some time telling her everything about the cute boy he got to live with for the next three weeks.

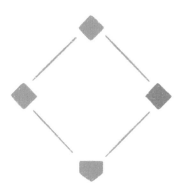

Taylor

At warm-ups the next morning, Taylor started to realize why Wil had seemed so lost when Jessie and Mateo were geeking out about baseball the previous day. Turned out he had no baseball skills at all. Like, at all.

Camp always started pretty slowly. The first day they just did stretches and started getting back into the swing of things. People would take turns batting and pitching, letting themselves fall into familiar routines.

Some folks were certainly rusty, but Wil seemed like he'd never been near a baseball before in his life. He couldn't even throw in a semi-straight line. Seeing him handle a bat was even worse—he held it like it might bite him without warning. Taylor honestly felt bad just watching him.

When Wil started walking out of the outfield towards the dugout, Taylor found himself wanting to follow. He called over someone he kind of knew from last year to take his spot playing catch and ducked away, jogging a bit to catch up to Wil.

"Hey, man. How's it going?" he started casually, sticking his hands in his pockets as they walked through the crowded field. He knew from experience that a lot of boys their age hated talking about their feelings, especially regarding things they weren't good at. He'd felt like they'd connected pretty well the previous day, but still they'd known one another less than twenty-four hours. It seemed best to keep it cool.

"You honestly have to ask?" Wil returned, snorting and raising an eyebrow. Taylor nodded, mostly to himself. Okay: a direct approach, then. "New to baseball?" he asked gingerly. The camp welcomed people of all ability levels. You didn't have to have any prior experience or anything. Still, most folks had at least played catch before.

"You don't say." Wil sighed. "I'm just not... a sports kind of guy." He shared, staring adamantly down at his newly refilled water bottle. "But my dad was really excited about this, so..." He trailed off, something that seemed to be a habit for him. It was the type of thing Taylor usually hated, but he thought he followed Wil well enough most of the time.

"Makes sense," he said. "Still, I'm sure you can figure it out. We were all new once." Taylor aimed for positive but not sappy, not really sure of how well that was actually coming across.

"Thanks." Wil shrugged, sitting down on the bench in the dugout. Taylor sat next to him. Wil continued, "I just... guys like me don't really play baseball, you know?"

Taylor most definitely did not know. He hated when people trailed off like this. No, sorry, what are you vaguely referring to? Did Wil mean nerdy guys or trans guys or small guys or some other thing he was assuming Taylor had picked up on but hadn't?

Regardless, one thing he did know with certainty: anyone who wanted to could darn well play baseball. So, he chose to take that tack.

"Nah. I don't know." He answered honestly. "Because, last I checked, there isn't a rule about who can and can't play baseball." He let some force into his tone. "People still think I'm not really a sports kind of guy. 'Cause, obviously fat kids can't play sports, right?"

"You're not..." Wil started, and Taylor quickly cut him off before he could finish.

"No. Don't." He shook his head. "I'm fat. Never said it was a bad thing." It got exhausting, people always jumping in to "reassure" him every time he mentioned his size. He was perfectly fine with his body, he didn't need the constant reminders that he wasn't supposed to be.

Luckily, Wil was nodding along, seeming to actually hear what he was saying. Which was truthfully a better reaction than most. "Sorry," he mumbled, but it seemed genuine.

"It's okay. Apology accepted," he returned, meaning it as well. "Anyways, the point is lots of people think I can't play baseball 'cause I'm fat or 'cause I'm Asian. And that's not true. No reason you can't play too."

Wil gave him a little half-smile. "Yeah. But you saw me out there, I'm absolute rubbish." He acknowledged sheepishly. "Can you honestly tell me that I'm cut out for this?"

Taylor turned towards him, looking the boy up and down for a moment, before landing on his face. "How can you know what you can do if you've never practiced or been taught? I'm not saying you're the next Carlos González, but I am telling you right now, you have skills and we'll figure out what they are," he promised.

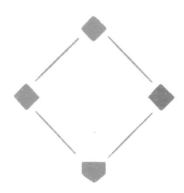

Wil

This would be the part where he tried desperately not to blush or squirm as Taylor's eyes trailed across him.

Carlos who? He thought. But Taylor's resolve caught him before he could worry too much about it. He was probably some kind of baseball player. "Okay. If you say so," he agreed awkwardly, still not believing he stood half a chance. But it was nice to at least feel a bit less alone.

"Come on, let's get back to the field." Taylor was already turning back. At least one of them was excited about this, Wil figured, before heading along after him.

Taylor stuck with him for the rest of the afternoon. It got hotter and hotter outside as time passed. There was absolutely no shade on the field. While Wil didn't necessarily improve with practice, it really was nice not to be out there sucking at everything alone. Besides, Taylor's optimism was reassuring. The guy was absolutely convinced that Wil could do well at some part of this whole baseball business.

They spent a while talking about all the different baseball positions. Taylor rambled eagerly about why they were each important and what they did and how it changed throughout the game, occasionally punctuating a point with a diagram drawn in the air that could just as well have been a Pokémon.

Wil was starting to understand why Taylor had been upset when Wil was dismissive of his own interests. It was clear that he was just as passionate about baseball as Wil was about any of his own favorite activities.

In fact, he found that he kind of enjoyed listening to Taylor talk about baseball, which was a first. And, yeah, it was partially because of how cute Taylor was. Hands going every which way as he explained one thing or another. Eyes sparkling. But there was also something about Taylor himself, the way he talked, like of course they were friends and of course he would help Wil after knowing each other for barely a day.

Despite all that, Wil still didn't really follow anything Taylor was saying. He listened, feeling like it would start to click eventually if he just focused, but that never happened. Finally, when people were starting to head back to the dorms to get ready for dinner, he owned up to it.

"Thank you. For real," he started, hoping his sincerity came through. "You didn't have to take all of this time to teach me. I'm sorry I'm still horrible." He ducked his head down, a gesture he couldn't seem to stop. "But, I also... I still don't understand any of this. I know you've been explaining. It's not your fault. I'm sorry. I feel stupid." He forced it out all in a rush, the words coming too fast once they started.

Taylor held up a hand, stopping him. Then he reached out, pausing with his hand held just above Wil's shoulder. He looked up, nearly meeting Wil's eyes, something Wil had started to notice was a pattern with the other boy. "This okay?" he asked.

Wil nodded, not trusting himself with words.

Taylor clapped his hand down on Wil's shoulder, warm and reassuring. "You're not stupid," he stated firmly. "And you don't have anything to apologize for." He spoke with complete resolve as if he believed it absolutely. Wil didn't quite believe it himself, but as they stood there, in shared silence, he still felt a bit better.

"Thank you." He spoke softly, after a long moment.

"The rules and everything... still don't make sense?" Taylor clarified, in a much more casual tone of voice.

"No," Wil confirmed, feeling hesitant and unsure again. "I still don't get when people can run and when they can't. Or how far they're allowed to go." He couldn't imagine that he would ever understand. He didn't know how he'd make it through camp if he wasn't able to get a handle on them somehow.

"Fair enough. I'll just need to figure out a different way to explain them." Taylor shrugged, still sounding completely chill. "We'll get there. For now, lunch?" he asked, nodding in the direction of the dining hall.

"Yeah." Wil agreed. And when they turned to walk back, he enjoyed that Taylor simply slid his arm around his shoulders and gave him a little half hug, rather than pulling away.

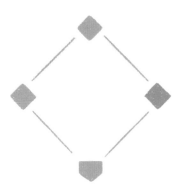

Taylor

"Tell me more about yourself?" he asked Wil, feeling thoughtful. They were back at Taylor's usual table in the dining hall, plates loaded with giant helpings of pasta.

Taylor had always liked puzzles. He was determined to figure out a way to explain baseball to the other boy. It had to be possible. And it felt... important. Not in the long run of things. But, for now, right here, Wil seemed so uncomfortable and so upset with himself.

Obviously, Taylor couldn't fully know why. But he got the impression that doing well, or at least decently, at baseball would help. So, it was worth figuring out. Plus, he liked Wil. He could see them becoming friends. They clicked well with one another.

"Uh, I don't know." Wil seemed startled, stopping with a fork full of noodles halfway to his mouth. Thus far they'd been eating in silence, Taylor completely caught up in his own thoughts.

"Do you need more specific questions?" Taylor asked. He often needed specificity himself, so he could understand that.

"No. At least I don't think so?" Wil seemed to be thinking it through, considering. "I think it's an okay question. I was just surprised."

"That's all right." Taylor smiled and shrugged. "Plenty of time."

"I don't really know what to say. I'm going into seventh grade. I'm a nerd; you knew that." He laughed. "I like Star Trek, D&D, board games, lots of other things. I'm playing a ranger in D&D right now and I'm running a different campaign too. I'm not usually very athletic. You probably knew that too. Usually in the summer I go to theater camp and I'm pretty sure they own some frisbees and jump ropes and stuff but I've never used it." He laughed again, and for once it didn't sound like he was laughing at himself.

"It's been just me and my dad since I was little. He's great, but we don't have much in common. He's the one who wanted me to come here. He seemed to really think I'd like it. Which is nice but like... there's a lot he doesn't really understand." Wil continued, more quietly now. Taylor got the impression he was being vulnerable.

"Thank you for sharing." He spoke honestly. They hadn't known one another long. He appreciated Wil's willingness to share so much with him.

"I wanna figure out a way to explain baseball that'll make more sense to you," Taylor commented. "Rattling off positions and statistics clearly isn't working. And, maybe it'll be easier to play when you understand it better. At the very least it should be less confusing." He pondered aloud, continuing to eat his lunch.

"It might take a bit, but we've got time," he repeated. After all, there were three weeks of camp stretching out in front of them. More than enough time to give Wil at least a rudimentary understanding of the sport. Maybe even get him really prepared for the end-of-summer game.

Wil

"What about you?" Wil asked after a moment, more than a bit taken aback by Taylor's apparent commitment to helping him. Sure, they were rooming together. But, they didn't really know each other. Taylor had no reason to help.

Plus, Taylor already had friends at camp. Wil knew that. Taylor had clearly known Jessie and Mateo for at least a bit. And, it was obvious that, unlike him, they didn't have any problems understanding baseball. Wil had gotten the impression that both of them played on teams themselves during the school year.

It was hard to understand why Taylor wanted to bother with him of all people. Still, Wil didn't have any other friends here. And, wasn't likely to make more if he couldn't even figure out the basics of the game, so he ought to be polite. Besides, he still liked Taylor, more than he cared to admit.

Taylor didn't need to consider the question the same way he had. "I'm going into seventh too." He shared over a bite of his food. "I love baseball." He didn't comment that Wil already knew that because of course he did. "I've been pitching since I was little. I run cross country too. And I listen to a lot of music."

Wil wasn't surprised that Taylor apparently did more than one sport. He seemed the type. The classic All-American boy. Tall, muscly, jock who would definitely rather be on a baseball field than on stage. Wil bitterly wondered if this is what his dad had secretly hoped for when he told him that he actually had a son before shaking his head to knock the thought away.

He knew it wasn't true. His dad had always loved him for who he was. He just didn't really know how to help him, Wil, his actual kid. He thought that sharing the things he'd liked as a boy with Wil would somehow affirm Wil's gender. It was well-meaning but often a bit off the mark.

"I live with my moms; I'm an only child." Wil was pulled back into the conversation there. "Moms." Well, maybe that explained why Taylor introduced himself with his pronouns. His parents were queer. "And, I'm autistic." Taylor continued, sharing that in the same tone of voice he'd used to state that he loved music.

Wil blinked. He wasn't used to people talking about disabilities as easily as that. Well, not anywhere except online. But Taylor didn't seem the slightest bit fazed.

"Cool." Wil managed after a minute. "I guess this camp is perfect for you." It certainly seemed like it. He could see how happy Taylor was here, especially when they'd been out on the field earlier in the day.

"Yeah," Taylor said cheerily, looking around the crowded dining hall. "I'd play baseball all day if I could. I've been coming here every summer for years. It's nice." He seemed reflective. "My moms aren't really sports people either." His eyes almost met Wil's again there, a wry commiserating look in them. "It's nice to be somewhere where people get me, you know?"

Wil looked out the nearby window at the trees in the green area outside, feeling suddenly wistful. He missed Camp Fletcher more than he could have imagined. He remembered cracking up with Leila during improv games, and trying to hold a serious expression in rehearsal while she made faces at him from the house. Theater camp had always been where he felt most understood. The one place he wasn't some kind of oddity. It was hard to be away from it now.

Taylor

Taylor wasn't certain how to read the expression on Wil's face, so he just let it be. He'd never been great at reading facial expressions. Years of social skills instruction and dissecting Star Trek episodes with his moms had helped, but he still missed or misunderstood as much as he caught. Taylor was pretty accustomed to ignoring things when that happened. He figured if something was really important to someone, they would bring it back up.

Wil seemed to stay reflective for a bit, eating his meal slowly, but he didn't say anything about it, so Taylor didn't either. He was fine with quiet. It could be easier than keeping up a constant conversation.

After lunch, they headed back out to the field for more practice. "Batting first?" Taylor proposed, turning toward home plate. "If that doesn't sound too scary." He was fully aware of how awful it could be to have a ball come right towards you from that distance. He hated it himself. But unless Wil ended up a pitcher too, he'd have to bat.

And, honestly, Taylor had seen Wil throw a ball. Sure, he would definitely improve, but there was also basically no way Wil was going to be a pitcher in the next three weeks. Which meant batting was non-optional, so they might as well start with it.

"Sure," Wil said.

"Okay, so start by grabbing a bat." Wil did so. "You're right handed?" Taylor asked. Wil nodded. "Cool. So then stand in this box." Taylor indicated the white rectangle painted on the dirt left of home base.

"Now, face this way and just hold the bat how you think you would if you were waiting for the pitch." Wil held up the bat cautiously, off-balance and looking like he might tip over if he tried to swing.

He definitely didn't have any good habits built up for his stance or grip of the bat, but at least he didn't have any bad ones either. Taylor could work with that. He spent a while circling Wil, looking at how he was holding his body, and suggesting adjustments. "How does that feel?"

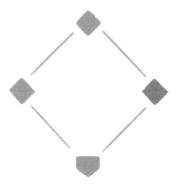

Wil

"Ummm, really awkward? This is a weird position to hold." Wil said, stiffly trying to stay exactly where Taylor had put him. His arms were starting to strain with the effort of holding the bat up.

"That's partly because you need to loosen up some. When you hit the ball, it takes a lot of force, and it's really easy to get thrown off balance. That's why your stance is so important. You don't want to get tipped over. You can relax now by the way." Wil let the bat drop to the ground and let out a long breath. He was glad to be out of that position.

"It's going to be easier to knock you over if you're standing stiff like that because there isn't any give for you to use to recover. Think about how easy it is to knock over a tower of Legos. If you're too stiff, you'll just tip over." Wil appreciated the visual. That actually kind of made sense.

"With your knees bent like that, you want to hold them loose, so you can shift your weight around." Taylor demonstrated, taking the same stance he had just put Wil in, but shifting his weight from one leg to the other and back, wiggling his butt, doing a jokey little dance as he got settled into his stance.

"Same with your arms. You know how batters waiting for the pitch will, like, wiggle the bat back and forth?" Wil shook his head. He was not familiar with this. The few times his dad had taken him to games, or when they were on TV, he had mostly messed around on his phone, flipping through TikToks with one earbud in or jotting down notes for the next session of his D&D campaign.

Taylor must have caught the blank look on his face. "Well, they do. Kind of like this." He demonstrated. "Watch tomorrow when other people are batting. You don't have much time to react to the pitch when you're batting, so you want to keep your muscles loose so you can swing faster. Try the stance again now."

Wil carefully attempted to recreate the position Taylor had just been in, feet apart, knees bent, elbows up. "Like this, yeah?"

"Really good. I would just slide your left foot forward a little." Wil did and then looked back at Taylor for approval. "Perfect, now try to loosen up, shift your weight around a bit." As Wil carefully moved his elbows and hips more he started to settle into the stance. It actually did feel really stable.

"Great!" Taylor said. "Okay, now for the actual swing." He walked up behind Wil and started to put his arms around him. "Is this okay?"

Wil felt his heart rate go up slightly as Taylor got closer. "Sure," he said, once again noticing the start of a blush creeping into his cheeks. Taylor put his hands gently over Wil's, and slowly guided the bat down and around.

"So this is how you swing. Try that a few times, and then I can throw you some pitches?"

Wil did his best, but he still felt awkward. He never seemed to swing at the right time. He literally didn't hit the ball once. Taylor tried to be reassuring, but still... it was hard not to doubt himself.

Taylor

Taylor was really impressed with how well Wil had picked up the batting stance. He definitely still needed a lot of practice, but for someone who was completely new he was doing great. Taylor had thrown some easy pitches for him, and while Wil didn't actually hit any, and still seemed really awkward holding the bat, he was definitely making progress.

Partway through the afternoon, Colin had rounded up their floor group and led everyone through some drills. They practiced throws and catches and running around the diamond. Taylor didn't get a chance to talk to Wil again until dinner when they met up with their plates of food at Taylor's favorite table in the dining hall.

Eventually, Jessie and Mateo came in as well. "Mind if I invite them to join us?" He asked Wil, seemingly startling him out of his thoughts. Wil looked up with some slight confusion and Taylor gestured at the pair. He didn't want to invite them over without Wil's consent. Not when he seemed to be in a bit of an odd headspace. Wil indicated that he didn't mind though, so Taylor waved them over once the two had their trays of food.

If he wasn't mistaken, he thought Wil was still a bit overwhelmed. He seemed to have a hard time with new people, but luckily Jessie could always be relied on to take over a conversation. It was a trait that Taylor had leaned on more than once himself.

Sure enough, she began chatting readily. Talking about the first full day of camp and how warm-ups had gone and what they thought might be served for breakfast tomorrow and her middle school baseball team and no end of other topics.

Taylor was smiling within a few minutes. He'd missed his friend. They lived on opposite halves of the state, so they didn't get to see one another often. She and Mateo both were out past the mountains in Grand Junction. They video called every so often and always for one another's birthdays. But it wasn't much.

He also found himself glancing over at Wil occasionally throughout the conversation, wanting to check that he wasn't feeling freaked out or like he couldn't get a word in edgewise or anything else of the sort. But he looked all right. Maybe not completely comfortable, but nothing seemed terribly off to Taylor.

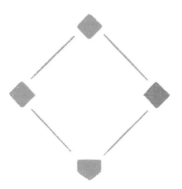

Wil

"Your friends seem cool," Wil said later that evening while he and Taylor walked back to their dorm. Taylor grinned happily at that. "I'm glad you like them," he said, seeming genuine, and once again Wil found himself somewhat taken aback at how much Taylor seemed to care.

"I love them." Taylor continued fondly. And then it was Wil's turn to smile. He didn't know a lot of boys who said they loved their friends. It was one of the things that made it harder to accept he really was a guy. He was emotional and affectionate and all sorts of things that it seemed like boys weren't supposed to be.

But Taylor clearly was. He was sweet and didn't shy away from physical contact or sharing how he felt. Plus, Wil had already seen him cry once, at the welcome back to camp show the counselors had surprised them with after dinner the previous night, and it definitely didn't seem like a rare occurrence. It was nice.

Thus far, the camp wasn't really shaping up to be as bad as he'd expected. Sure, he wasn't any good at baseball. But Taylor did have a point that this was his first day ever playing, there was only so much he could expect from himself.

And, more importantly, it didn't seem like being bad at baseball was the end of the world. Or like everyone else here was going to be a jerk to him just because they were jocks. Not everyone had been as nice as Taylor, but even before they started working together, no one had said anything mean.

He'd been so scared that he wouldn't fit in here. That he'd be surrounded by a bunch of athletic cis guy jerks and would never make friends. That he'd be lucky to escape without being terribly bullied. But as of yet, none of those fears seemed likely to come true.

Quite the opposite in fact. And actually, he was finding it kind of nice to be in an environment that was mostly other boys. Contrary to all of his expectations. Maybe his dad hadn't been completely off base after all. Even if his approach was a little skewed.

Off base. Huh. He wondered if that was a baseball metaphor. Maybe Taylor would know.

"Off base?" Taylor replied a bit distractedly. "I guess it probably is related to baseball. Haven't ever really thought about it." Taylor weighed his twenty-sided die in his hand, feeling it warm up gradually. Uncertain what to hope for. They'd be drawing teams soon. It was always random, though Taylor suspected the counselors did some fine-tuning after the fact to ensure each team got kids familiar with each position.

It would be great to be on a team with Wil. But it would be fine if they weren't on the same team. They could still practice together. And it was always fun getting to watch his friends' games. At this point, he honestly just wanted a decision. Taylor hated uncertainty; it made it hard to settle his brain.

He tossed the die back and forth between his hands rapidly, trying to force his thoughts onto another topic. "Is that a D20?" Wil asked with obvious surprise. Taylor nodded in confirmation, catching it in one hand and passing it over to Wil.

"I thought you didn't play?" Wil accepted the die, letting it roll into his palm as he registered the weight of it. "It's metal," he observed. Taylor nodded again.

"I don't particularly play." He shrugged, fingers tapping steadily against the center of his hand now that he'd handed over the die. "It's a stim more than anything else." He explained, needing a long moment to realize that had clarified nothing for Wil.

"I like how it feels. It's a good sensory thing," he expanded.
"I stole my Nanay's often enough when I was little that they bought me my own." Taylor smiled at the memory. At all the memories really, his mind jumping from one to the next. Wil nodded and passed the die back to him.

"They?" he asked, something in his eyes that Taylor couldn't read.

"My Nanay, my parent" he replied, well used to these sorts of questions. His Nanay's pronouns often confused people. Taylor grabbed a photo off his dresser, one of the ones Ma gave him before camp. He knew she couldn't resist the urge to decorate his room some since he had no intention of doing so himself.

"That's Nanay." He pointed them out. Though Nanay looked so much like him that people never guessed they could be anything but related. "They're genderqueer." He rather doubted he'd have to explain that one to Wil, though goodness knew he was prepared to if he did. He'd been getting those types of questions since he was three.

"Really?" Wil's delight was more apparent there. "That's so cool." He took the photo, looking closer. Taylor let him. "I've never even met another trans person before." Wil sat down next to Taylor, still studying the picture. Taylor made space for him, waiting to see if Wil said anything more.

Wil had said "another." Taylor already suspected he was trans, but that seemed like confirmation of it. A part of him wanted to thank Wil for sharing, but it didn't seem to fit the conversation. "Well, you'll meet my moms soon," he said cheerily instead.

"They always come to my game on family weekend." Not that they followed any of it. But they cheered when everyone else did and were unfailingly proud of him afterward. "Honestly, you've probably met plenty of trans folks before and just didn't know it," he couldn't help but add, thinking of some of his own family members people were always surprised to learn were trans.

"Good point," Wil said happily. He'd never really considered that before, but it seemed obvious now. He liked the thought. That he might not be the only trans person here. Or anywhere really. That there were lots of others out there that he just didn't know that well.

"I guess your moms are pretty open?" he asked, remembering the bumper sticker he'd spotted the first day of camp. In retrospect, it seemed likely that it had been Taylor's family's car.

"Yeah." Taylor nodded with a slight chuckle. "They're about as loud and proud as it comes." He rolled his eyes, but it seemed affectionate.

Wil wondered what it would have been like to grow up like that. "I'm kind of jealous," he admitted after a moment.

Taylor nodded seriously. "That's valid," he said. "Tell me about your family?" he asked after a minute, the prompt gentle and a bit hesitant.

Wil paused, thinking. "Like I've said, it's just my dad and me," he started fondly, missing his dad already. "He's great. Kind of overprotective sometimes, but I know that it's just that he loves me. Also, I probably got my anxiety from him," Wil observed with a laugh. His dad got every bit as worried about things as he did. "Otherwise, I don't know. He's kind of traditional? He played baseball growing up, that's why I'm here." He shrugged. "He's a tool and die maker."

It was weird realizing how little he really knew about the man. Everyone he'd been friends with in elementary school just knew his dad. Wil had never really had to tell anyone about him before. "What position did he play?" Taylor asked curiously, making conversation.

"I... have no idea," Wil responded. He'd never thought to ask. He made a mental note to ask the next time his dad called. He wanted to learn more about him.

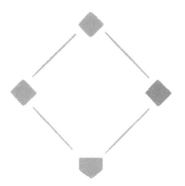

Taylor

That evening Taylor was up late, back to thinking about baseball, his mind still spinning way too quickly through every possibility about positions and teams rosters. Rolling his die at the tips of his fingers in familiar patterns. Teams getting decided was always the first part of camp that made everything really come into focus. They were no longer just messing around; there were games to be played.

Taylor was the first person to admit that he got invested. He had to work hard to not be a sore loser, and he was fiercely competitive. On the mound, he fell into the kind of single-minded determination he only had with the things he really cared about.

It was as exciting as it was nerve-racking to realize that their first game was only a few days off. Camp always flew by so quickly. They'd feel like proper teams before he knew it. Three games and three weeks went by faster than you'd think.

And he'd still made absolutely no progress explaining the game to Wil, for all that he'd tried more than once. It was beginning to feel reminiscent of teaching his Nanay, except unlike them, Wil had an actual reason to learn. Repeating the same things endlessly wouldn't do a thing though. He needed a new approach.

He was positive Wil would actually like it once he got it. At the end of the day baseball was half numbers; that was part of what Taylor liked about it. It was a structured sport. Predictable. You may not be able to anticipate the results of a game, but each at-bat had a limited number of possible outcomes. Taylor appreciated that about it. He thought Wil would too.

Wait. He grabbed his die and squeezed it, corners pressing into his skin. That was it. D&D. He laughed out loud before remembering what time it was and trying to be quieter. He grabbed a notebook out of his backpack, turned on his reading light, and started brainstorming. That could really work.

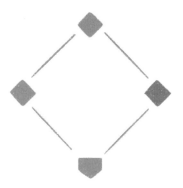

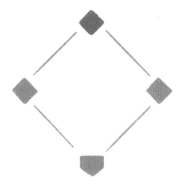

Part Two

Wil

"D&D?" Wil felt dubious, to say the least. Taylor was cute when he was excited, hands and arms swinging back and forth as he explained his idea. "Yeah. D&D. It's perfect," Taylor exclaimed ecstatically.

"Here. Just listen." He seemed to register Wil's doubt. "If it still doesn't make sense, that's fine. But I think it will. That's all," he tried to reassure. Wil appreciated it. He already felt guilty that Taylor had spent so much time on him, all trying to explain the same thing over and over again. It was hard not to feel like a burden.

"You play a ranger, right?" Wil was impressed that Taylor remembered. He knew that D&D wasn't really his thing. "Yeah. A Tiefling ranger." Taylor nodded in acknowledgment. "Tell me about them?" Wil still didn't really see how that related to baseball, but he was always happy to talk about Reina.

"She's a Tiefling ranger, level 7." Wil wasn't certain how much of his explanation Taylor would understand, but he was listening attentively anyway, so he continued. "Uses a longbow. Her favored enemy is undead, like zombies and vampires." He was grinning now. D&D was on hold for the summer and he missed his party. It was nice getting to talk about his character at least.

"Longbow is a ranged weapon, so she likes to find cover and shoot from a distance." Wil was just rambling now, uncertain what else to say. "Is that the kind of stuff you wanted to know?" he asked, not at all sure where Taylor had been heading with the question. Taylor looked thoughtful, fingers dancing together as he listened.

"Yeah. That's perfect. Thanks," he said with a happy grin. Wil fought back a blush. Taylor was entirely too cute like this, all excited about an idea.

"So, I have it all mapped out. I think I can explain baseball to you using D&D."

Taylor was repeating himself, but Wil didn't care. "Just stop me if anything doesn't make sense and I can try again?" Wil nodded his agreement, still dubious but less so. Taylor's optimism really was contagious.

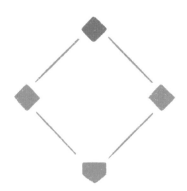

Taylor

"So, I'm really just trying to explain the rules of baseball." Taylor had to clarify, realizing all at once how none of his explanations actually related to the rules of D&D. "I'm using D&D terminology, but none of it would really work in-game. Does that make sense?" He waited for Wil's serious nod before continuing.

"Batting is like a contested dexterity check with the pitcher." Taylor started, notebook in front of him. "So, the pitcher, that's me, and the batter are competing. They're trying to do different things. It's like playing tag, where one person is trying to tag and the others are dodging." He stood up. "The pitcher is trying to throw the ball where the batter could reasonably hit it, but it would be hard to do so. And the batter is trying to hit the ball." Taylor mimed each action as he explained.

Wil was watching with an expression Taylor couldn't parse. "Does that make sense?" Taylor checked in. It worked in his mind, but he had the advantage of being familiar with both D&D and baseball to start. "Yeah. It actually does." Wil seemed surprised, and Taylor smiled at him, happy that his idea was working out.

"You know how in D&D each turn lasts six seconds?" Wil nodded again, smiling himself. "In baseball, each turn is one batter's attempt at bat. And, that turn can end one of two ways. The batter is either safe or out." Luckily some baseball language was decently intuitive. Taylor figured the terms safe and out explained themselves fairly well.

"An out is basically just taking damage, though obviously players don't get injured because of it. Hopefully." He laughed. He'd missed half his season when he was nine because of a strained shoulder. He still remembered how upset he'd been about it.

"Are you still following?" He had to ask again, still feeling uncertain of himself. It definitely wouldn't be the first time he thought he was communicating really well, but the other person was completely confused. Or worse yet, they thought they understood, but everything he was trying to say was actually getting entirely muddled.

"I think so. If the batter is safe, they're still in the game. And if they're out they sit back down and don't have any chance of scoring." Wil reiterated. "Yeah. That's right." Taylor agreed with a happy smile. It seemed like they really were on the same page this time.

"What else?" Wil asked, leaning forward. And that was more reassuring than anything else. Wil wanted to know more. He wasn't just listening because he thought he should. He was actually asking Taylor to go on.

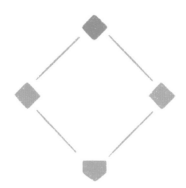

Wil

Wil had been starting to accept that this would just never make sense. He'd be stuck here for almost a month, and, sure, it wasn't as awful as he'd expected. But it would still be a waste of time. No matter how long he stayed or how many times Taylor patiently explained the game, he still wouldn't understand it.

It was a surprise to realize that he maybe could. And that made him want to hear even more. "Now, I'm going to talk about the bases, okay?" Taylor informed him, showing him one of the doodles he'd drawn in his notebook. Wil remembered what the bases were, four points around the square. Sorry, diamond.

"So, bases are kind of like cover." Taylor started and Wil had to smile. He wondered if this was part of the original explanation or something Taylor came up with once he'd started talking about Reina. "Being on base is like total cover. If you're touching one you can't be targeted."

"So, if you're on base you can't get out?" Wil started putting the pieces together. This really wasn't as incomprehensible as he'd once thought.

"Exactly," Taylor replied, "A batter can try to make it as far as they want, but if they leave base they no longer have cover until they reach the next one."

Taylor continued, tracing around the illustration he'd drawn as he talked.

Wil followed his finger, watching the route the batter would have to take around the baseball diamond. It seemed like it would be pretty easy to make it to first, but a lot harder to run further. "And cover is called being safe?" He remembered the term from Taylor's endless earlier baseball explanations.

"That's right." Taylor looked proud. "If the batter gets tagged by someone holding the ball, they're out. So, the farther they hit it, the further they might be able to run. You just have to avoid getting tagged. "

Wil thought he followed. "Cool. So, when you bat you hit the ball and then run as far as you can before someone gets the ball back to you?" he clarified.

"Exactly." Taylor grinned. "Though, I'd rather not be at bat myself." He chuckled. "I hate things coming towards me suddenly. That's part of why I like pitching. I'd rather throw the ball to someone else than have it coming at me." Wil nodded, processing that.

It kind of surprised him to realize that Taylor wasn't just perfect at all aspects of baseball. It had felt like that mostly because Wil knew absolutely nothing about the sport and Taylor had played it for years. There was something reassuring about realizing that even Taylor had parts he didn't like as much.

"I have no idea what position I could play," Wil said. A key difference was that there were parts that Taylor did like and was good at, in stark contrast to himself.

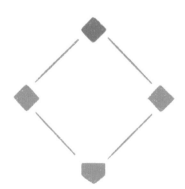

Taylor

"Hey, Wil." Taylor reached out, seeking permission to touch him. Wil nodded consent, and Taylor took his hand in what he hoped was a comforting manner, holding it between them. "You've never played before. Nobody starts knowing what's going to be the best fit for them." He could tell how much Wil doubted himself and he wished there was some way he could change that.

The best he could do was keep offering reassurance though. At the end of the day, Wil would have to find that confidence on his own. "We can figure positions out together," he promised, knowing that at least this was something he could help with, even if there was little he could do to build up Wil's self-confidence.

Wil nodded, but didn't say anything. Taylor figured that was at least better than him continuing to say things that undermined himself. They sat together in silence for a while longer before finally getting corralled back towards the dining hall for dinner.

After dinner that evening, they headed back to their room, bypassing all of the optional activities without needing to confer about it. Taylor still was having trouble focusing on anything other than baseball. And Wil's thoughts seemed to be elsewhere.

They both relaxed in relative quiet for a bit, before Wil finally broke the silence, sounding like he was sharing something that had been on his mind for a while. "Do you..." he started, before stopping. "You touch people more than any other guy I know," he stammered out after a moment.

Taylor listened curiously, nodding in agreement. But Wil's face was flushing. "Not... I mean, just touch. You know, like holding hands and hugs and things like that," he clarified a bit frantically. Taylor wondered what he was so worried about.

"Yeah. I like physical contact." Taylor agreed simply. "And I grew up with a lot of it." He didn't know what had brought this up, but it was clearly a topic that Wil had thought a lot about. His responses came slowly as if he needed time to get his words together.

"I didn't think I could have that kind of thing if I was a boy. I mean, if I came out," he managed after a long moment and Taylor finally thought he understood. "Most guys don't really..." Wil trailed off, but Taylor was fairly certain he had an idea where Wil was going.

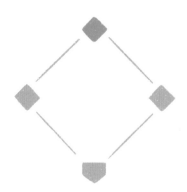

Wil

Wil had absolutely no clue why he'd brought this up. In what universe is talking about physical contact with your crush a good idea? But he couldn't stop thinking about it. How Taylor's hand felt in his. Or how nice it was to have Taylor's arm around his shoulders. Not even just because Wil liked him, but because it was nice to be properly recognized as a guy and still allowed that. He'd been so scared he was giving up that closeness, that love, when he came out.

"Isn't..." He tried to find the right words. "Isn't it different when you're a guy though?" he asked hesitantly. He didn't want to sound too unsure. Didn't want to sound like he wasn't really a boy. Wasn't he supposed to already understand this stuff? But he didn't.

Taylor looked thoughtful, D20 in his hands again. Now that Wil knew what it was, it was easy to spot. It was there more often than not. He wondered what about it it was that Taylor liked specifically. He'd have to ask sometime.

"It is." Taylor agreed after a long moment, looking out into space. Wil was beginning to notice that the more serious the topic of conversation, the less likely Taylor was to try to make eye contact or even really to look at him. Now that he understood, he didn't mind it. He knew that Taylor was attentive nonetheless.

"I grew up with a lot of physical contact. Hugs and kisses and giant, queer cuddle puddles," Taylor said with a fond-sounding laugh. "We try to check in, but there's a lot of ongoing consent. And most everyone is here for it." Wil thought he'd enjoy having a family like that; it wasn't at all what he was used to.

"I like all of that." Taylor continued. "But, yeah, I do think that things are different for guys." He spoke slowly. "It didn't matter so much when I was little. But now..." Taylor looked down at himself. "I grew almost a foot in the past year alone. I'm a big guy.

"Now that I'm older, that makes a difference too. It feels like people are a bit more hesitant around me sometimes. You know?" Wil remembered suddenly how intimidated he'd been by Taylor when they first met. Before he had a chance to realize what a sweetheart he actually was. Yeah. He could understand that.

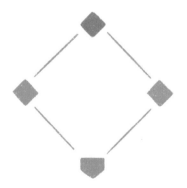

Taylor

Taylor sighed. It was messy. And this stuff was hard to talk about. He hadn't ever tried with his moms. And most of his friends back home hadn't grown up in the same kind of environment he had. He didn't know if any of them would understand.

Really, he didn't have any reason to assume that Wil would understand either. But he'd asked and that was enough to make it worth discussing. "I've started to be extra careful," Taylor found himself explaining.

"I try to ask. Every time before I touch someone. Unless they're my parent or someone else I have clear ongoing consent for that with." He'd never consciously connected these thoughts before.

"And I try to make certain I don't push into people's space. That I'm not too close," he continued. "Though, I'm cautious about that. There's a lot of fatphobic talk out there that basically says I don't deserve to take space at all," he scoffed.

"That's wrong. But still manspreading is a thing, and pressing into people's personal space isn't okay. I try to walk a line there. I don't think I always get it right." He shrugged. He was figuring it out as he went. A lot of the time he felt pretty lost.

It was tricky. And he'd never been fantastic at reading people. If he wasn't so hyper-intentional about watching body language, he might never have caught the way some folks had started shying away from him at all.

He always felt like he had to pay conscious attention, because nonverbal communication wasn't something he understood naturally. But even still, though he'd noticed that change, he couldn't necessarily read the nuances.

"Boys can touch though." Taylor felt the need to assert, looping back to the original topic. "There's nothing wrong with it. We deserve physical contact, that kind of affection, as much as anyone else. Assuming we want it. And nothing about being a boy means that isn't possible. You just have to find the right people."

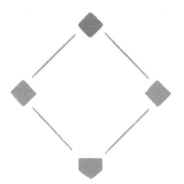

Wil

Wil listened attentively. He was kind of in awe of Taylor, sharing all of that with him. It felt vulnerable. And, that made it special. Wil didn't think that people really reacted to him differently like that right now. He was a lot smaller than Taylor. People still mostly saw him as a child. *And sometimes a girl,* he mentally acknowledged with frustration.

Wil wondered if his own masculinity would impact people like that someday. And he wondered if it could happen without him even noticing it. He could imagine that. He was so comfortable in the notion that he was a safe person that he might not even notice the impact he had on someone who didn't know him. He resolved to be careful of that.

"Thank you." He felt comforted by Taylor's reassurance. "I do like touch. It makes me feel safe and loved and it's just nice." He reached for Taylor's hand, suddenly craving that contact.

"Being a boy feels complicated sometimes," Wil shared. "There are so many little factors and nuances in how people see me. I never really know who to talk to about it." He felt like he could talk with Taylor. That was something new.

"I never know if it's because I'm trans or if everyone feels like this." He shrugged, not voicing that sometimes it made him worry he wasn't really trans. It could be hard not to feel like in order to actually be a boy, he had to understand everything about what that meant.

Taylor squeezed his hand. "I don't think that everyone experiences it the same." He spoke softly. "Like how you don't have to think about being fat or Filipino and how those pieces affect things the same way I do," he offered as an example.

"I don't really understand the trans aspect of it." Taylor acknowledged. "But masculinity. Being a guy. Yeah. I think that's tough for everyone," Taylor mused. "In different ways, but still it's complex. I wish people talked about that more." Wil nodded in agreement. He felt like he needed someone with more experience, someone who could help him figure out that kind of thing.

It took a moment before he realized that his dad could be a good person for that. Sure, they weren't completely the same, but for sure he'd navigated some of what Wil was thinking about now.

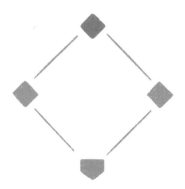

Taylor

After their conversation, they'd gone to bed early. Taylor had found himself oddly worn out from the more serious direction their talk had gone. And probably from the lack of sleep the previous evening.

But that morning, all of his swirling thoughts were back again. Team rosters would be announced at lunch. He knew there was no reason to be this concerned about them. It wasn't like he really cared who was on which team. And yet he couldn't make his mind calm down.

He was up early, pacing back and forth through their small dorm room, trying to do so as quietly as possible. He felt like he couldn't sit still. But he wanted to go to breakfast with Wil when he woke up. Besides, they weren't allowed to leave the residence hall by themselves this early anyways.

Once Wil woke, Taylor spent much of the morning pulling up clips of baseball games on his phone, showing them to Wil, and expanding his understanding of the game. It kept Taylor's mind occupied, and Wil seemed to appreciate the further explanation.

Still, by the time they were headed to lunch, Taylor was completely caught up in his own thoughts again, unable to pull himself out of them enough to really talk about anything. Even baseball.

Wil seemed to register where he was at. "Nervous?" he asked, nudging Taylor's shoulder lightly. Taylor leaned into the contact gladly.

"Just thinking about team rosters," he explained, not bothering to clarify that he was less nervous than simply caught up in anticipation.

"Fair," Wil acknowledged as they made their way into the

dining hall together. Rosters wouldn't actually be shared until everyone was pretty much finished eating, so Taylor had a whole meal to get through before he had any kind of certainty.

They found Jessie and Mateo at their usual spot, and Taylor sank down gratefully, glad to be out of the chaotic buffet lines. The two were bickering companionably about something, and Taylor happily let them lead the conversation, fidgeting steadily while he slowly ate.

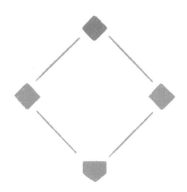

Wil

Wil was worried about Taylor but didn't have any idea how to support him. The other boy had gone quiet, so he tried to let him be, simply shooting concerned glances in his direction every so often. He wondered what Taylor was so nervous about.

The rosters weren't something he'd thought much about before now. Sure, they all got assigned to teams. But the games weren't that big a deal, were they? It was just summer camp. Then again, Wil didn't really know anything about this kind of summer camp.

Jessie got up to get some more food and Wil excused himself at the same time, edging closer to the tall girl as they wove between food stations. "Hey, do you think Taylor's okay?" he asked, a bit nervously, but feeling mostly okay. Jessie was nice, and he was fairly comfortable with her by now. And he'd always been less nervous around girls than guys.

"Taylor?" Jessie repeated, glancing back in the direction they'd come from. "Yeah. I'm sure he's fine." She spoke lightly. "Taylor always gets all antsy before rosters come out. He takes all this way too seriously." She laughed but didn't seem judgemental, just amused. "I think it's his secret. Treat every game like it's part of the World Series."

Wil nodded. That made sense. When Taylor cared about something, he was fiercely passionate about it. Wil had seen that more than once by now. And baseball seemed to be the thing he cared about more than anything else. Of course, he got super invested in it.

Taylor remained quiet for the rest of lunch, but Wil was less worried about it now, even allowing himself to be drawn into the conversation some. Mateo decided they were the perfect audience for some of the most ridiculously dorky-sounding baseball jokes he'd ever heard.

And Wil felt he had to counter with some equally dorky theater jokes of his own. It helped that Jessie and Mateo seemed amused by them, even if they were occasionally confused. Just like he was by some of Mateo's baseball jokes.

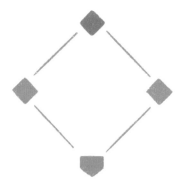

Taylor

"Can I get a drum roll, please?" Colin announced, leading to most of the camp banging on their tables. This was why Taylor preferred to sit in the corner. Whatever happened to being respectful of the other groups? But no one really seemed bothered.

"Introducing... Coach Rose!" Coach climbed onto a chair with one sturdy step and an amused expression. "Settle down," she reminded the campers after a minute, waiting for everyone to fall quiet before continuing.

"I know that you all have been eagerly awaiting team rosters." She looked around the room at that, and Taylor got the impression that she'd been fielding questions all morning. "They'll be posted in the dugouts when you return to the field this afternoon. At 1:00 you'll be meeting with your team at the location listed on the roster. Don't be late."

It was a familiar routine for many of the kids, who had started chowing down on any remaining food the moment Coach Rose got up to speak. "You're dismissed," she announced after a final moment, sparking a mass exodus from their corner of the dining hall, everyone eager to see who they'd be playing with.

Taylor hung back, like usual. He was as antsy for the rosters as anyone else, maybe more so. But his dislike of too many people all moving at once was even greater. Wil stayed with him this time, and he appreciated the company, following the group at a more sedate pace a few minutes after they'd left.

"You two are on the same team," Mateo called out across the crowd as they began to approach the dugout. Taylor nodded, taking in the information, but still determined to get to the paper and see for himself everyone on the team. He'd timed it well, as the group of kids still pressed close was starting to thin out and he could get in more easily.

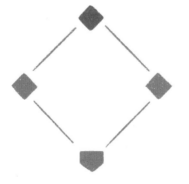

Wil

"Woo!" Wil started to exclaim, cutting himself off as Taylor continued to press forward, seemingly not even registering Wil's excitement. He'd been hoping to get put on the same team as Taylor but tried not to get his hopes up too much. He knew that there would be four teams, and apparently, the process of assigning them was mostly random.

It would be so much fun to get to hang out with Taylor all summer. Even if he never did figure out what he was doing, at least their practices would be together. It would be way worse to be awful and stuck on a team without anyone he really knew.

He looked around him at the swarm of campers excitedly chattering and starting to break up into groups. Some celebrated together or high-fived, excited to be on the same team. Others were disappointed to be separated from their friends. But there was an undercurrent of excitement. Team rosters seemed to be prompting a real start to the main part of camp.

Taylor didn't seem to share that excitement though. He'd barely even responded to Mateo's comment. Wil tried not to be disappointed by that. They were still on a team together. That was what counted.

"What about you two?" he forced himself to ask, catching up with Mateo and Jessie where they stood towards the edge of the field.

"We're split up," Jessie said with obvious disappointment. "I swear they do it on purpose." She sounded annoyed.

"Come on, you know it's random." Mateo jostled her lightly. "You just hate knowing that my team is going to beat yours." He teased with a smirk.

"Wanna bet?" Jessie replied, full of energy again. And, the two were off, easy as that, arguing happily with one another.

Wil looked into the dugouts towards Taylor, who was studiously reading over the entire roster. He supposed he might as well head over and see where their team was supposed to meet that afternoon. He didn't particularly care about who else was with them though. It wasn't like he was likely to recognize most of the names.

"Hey." Taylor greeted Wil as he approached, not looking up from the list of names. He had a neutral expression and seemed more focused and determined than excited. Was he worried that Wil would drag his team down? "We should get in some position practice over the next couple of days. Figure out where you're going to fit best," he suggested.

"Uhh, sure. I'm excited we're on the same team." Wil smiled genuinely. He was probably worried for no reason. And he did like spending time with Taylor.

Taylor nodded his agreement. "Me too. It'll be fun." He stole one last glance at the roster before starting to head out to the field to meet with the team.

Their team's coach was named Alyx, a perky, cheerful girl whom he was pretty positive was Jessie and Mateo's floor leader. Wil liked Alyx. She was one of the only counselors at camp who was a girl, and she'd been super patient with all of his dad's questions at check-in. He was happy to have her coaching their team.

She introduced herself with her usual upbeat attitude before leading the whole group in some standard get-to-know-you games. Wil looked over at Taylor. He still wished that Taylor had seemed happier to be on a team together in the first place, but he tried to shake the feelings off.

The rest of the day seemed to go quickly. There was no time for unstructured practice that afternoon. Instead, the focus was on team bonding. They barely even did anything directly baseball-related, which Wil supposed he should be happy about, but he was already getting nervous for their first game.

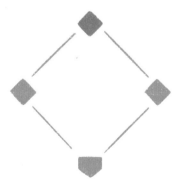

Taylor

The next morning, Taylor only nodded to his friends as they arrived for breakfast. His brain raced with thoughts about the upcoming game. "I was thinking it might be good to spend the next couple of mornings just playing around with different positions and seeing what might be the best fit for you?" he suggested. The assistant coaches always gave people a bit of time to try different positions before they made a final plan. Less experienced players, like Wil, definitely needed it.

Mornings at the camp were typically reserved for unstructured individual practice. As long as they were warmed up by the afternoon, the coaches didn't really care what they worked on. Besides, Alyx was easygoing. Taylor definitely liked her. She was sweet and easy to talk to and he was ninety percent certain she was queer. But she didn't tend to focus a lot on strategy or go overboard with team practice. She wouldn't mind them working on their own thing in the mornings.

He was pulled out of his thoughts when he realized Wil had yet to respond. Looking across the table, Taylor registered that he seemed fairly lost in thought himself. "Everything good?" he asked casually, wondering where Wil's mind was.

Wil's eyes darted up with a half-surprised expression. "Yeah. I'm just worried about the game," he shared, beginning to spoon cereal towards his mouth again.

Taylor nodded in agreement. "Me too." He sighed, already on edge.

"We didn't even start practice yesterday. We're all going to have to do a lot of work to be ready." Taylor's thoughts drifted back towards who might play what position. "Did you hear me earlier?" he inquired. "I suggested we spend some time figuring out your position."

Wil nodded seriously. "Yeah. I guess I need to. I really don't know what I'd be good at." He sighed, eyes dropping down again. "I have terrible aim. You've seen that." He shrugged. "And I get freaked out any time the ball comes near me."

Taylor reached out and squeezed his hand. "Me too," he reminded. "We'll figure it out."

Wil

Wil refrained from pointing out that it wasn't quite the same. Taylor just didn't like things flying towards his face. Wil didn't actually mind that too much, at least not more than the average person. He just always second-guessed what to do, freezing up deciding whether to swing and then wildly swinging too early when he tried to avoid that.

Wil hadn't even gotten batting down and Taylor already wanted to add in position practice. Wil had been worried about being rubbish during the game and everyone judging him for it. But it was clear that Taylor was just worried about losing. And not on his own account. Wil may not be close with any of the other campers, but that didn't mean he was oblivious to what they said.

Taylor was one of the best pitchers at camp. More than one person had remarked on it. And Jessie had said how seriously he took these games. He was probably disappointed to be on the same team as Wil. It had been silly to expect him to be happy about it.

Taylor wanted to win. And Wil was the biggest liability here. Taylor was right. He didn't even know what position he could play. He'd only just started really understanding the concept of the game this morning. How on earth was he supposed to be prepared to play sometime this weekend?

Especially since this was a thing Taylor and plenty of others on the team seemed to really care about. It obviously wasn't nearly as casual as Wil had originally assumed. Nothing like the lighthearted skits they'd put on at theater camp. Silly things that were about practicing new skills and amusing themselves, but nothing serious.

Sure, everything had gone all right so far, but that was because the actual baseball part of baseball camp hadn't properly started yet. Now that it had, all of Wil's fears were rushing back again. No wonder Taylor was already scheming trying to find some way to make him slightly less awful. Wil supposed he should still appreciate the attention.

Besides, it was perfectly clear that Taylor really was a nice guy. Here he was, squeezing Wil's hand, reassuring him. They were still friends. That hadn't changed.

It just didn't feel like the coaching was solely about that. Baseball was a priority to Taylor. And Wil was well-positioned to mess with that.

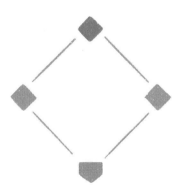

"Okay. So each position is really in place just to help get out any runners." Taylor explained once they reached the field. "You remember how that works?" he checked in. Wil seemed to have a decent grasp on things by now, but Taylor still didn't want to assume.

"Yeah. I think so." Wil nodded, looking intent. "Once the batter hits the ball they have to try to make it all the way around and back to home without getting tagged by the ball." He spoke slowly, seeming like he was seeking out the right words as he went. Taylor nodded, impressed.

"Yes, exactly. A batter is also out if their ball is caught before it hits the ground," he added, waiting for Wil's nod of understanding once he'd processed the new information. "So, the main goals are catching and throwing. And some running to get to where a ball is going to land."

"So, if it's all the same skills, how do they decide who's best in each position?" Wil asked after a long moment looking out across the pitch.

"It's mostly a question of what distance you throw and catch best from," Taylor explained.

"Okay." Wil looked determined, though there was something more there that Taylor couldn't quite read. "Catching and throwing then?" he proposed, and Taylor nodded. That had been his plan for this morning. Thus far they'd mostly focused on batting, but Wil would need to be able to play defensively too.

"You'll need a glove," Taylor remembered suddenly, already starting to make his way towards the gym where loaner equipment was stored. Wil jogged after him for a couple of paces, catching up. "Wait. I have my own." He veered towards the dormitories instead.

"You do?" Wil chuckled at Taylor's obvious surprise. It was cute.

"It was my dad's," he clarified.

"Ah, cool." Taylor grinned at that. Wil shot him a smile in return. "That's really awesome." Taylor continued. "I would have loved to have something passed down, but no one in my family is really into sports." He shrugged, looking a bit wistful.

"I don't think my dad ever really expected I'd have a chance to use it." Wil shared in return. "But, he always took care of it anyway. I think baseball was really important to him growing up." His dad wasn't typically very talkative when he wasn't fussing over Wil, but the few times he did tell stories about his childhood they had to do with baseball as often as not. Wil had heard more of them over the past few months.

That felt special now in retrospect. Though at the time Wil had been all nerves, and hearing about everything his dad and "the boys" did when they were young had only increased his anxiety. Now that everything felt less scary, Wil could appreciate the pieces of his childhood that his dad had shared.

"Let's see this glove," Taylor spoke excitedly the moment they were back to their room, pulling Wil out of his memories. Wil pulled it out of a drawer of his dresser, baseball still nestled carefully inside of it. Wil didn't really understand why that was important, but his dad had been clear that it was.

"Your dad took good care of this," Taylor observed, examining it carefully. Wil had already seen how careful Taylor was with his own glove, carefully cleaning it each evening. It was a practice he was already familiar with from his dad, who conditioned his own glove once a season like clockwork.

"It's not actually a glove though," Taylor shared casually. "It's a mitt." Wil looked over, curious. He hadn't actually realized that there was a difference between the two. He'd always assumed that the terms were used interchangeably. "Your dad must have been a catcher. Or a first baseman."

Wil nodded, glad now that he'd asked last time they talked. "Catcher," he shared, pleased that he knew. Taylor nodded knowingly. "He must have been a good one," he remarked. "He clearly loved the game." Wil nodded again. He'd never doubted that.

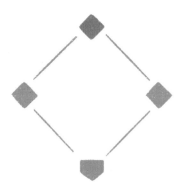

Taylor

They spent the next couple of mornings practicing throwing and catching. Wil turned out to be better at catching, though he wasn't great at either. Even with Taylor coaching him through all of the motions the best that he could, Wil just... lacked the experience that most of the kids here had. He couldn't throw very far and was very rarely anywhere on target. His throws were all over the place too, inconsistently going too far to one side or the other.

When Friday morning arrived, Alyx directed everyone to focus on batting practice, taking turns using the batting cages behind the field. Taylor hated this, but at least he was able to get it over with quickly before yielding his spot to newer players who needed more practice. He spent some time watching Wil bat. His form was a lot better, even though he still hesitated and swung late a lot of the time.

Once everyone had gotten a turn, with some extra time allotted to new players, they walked as a group to the dining hall for lunch. Alyx would be announcing their positions for the first game following lunch, so there was little else they could do for the time being. He was curious where she'd place Wil though. He understood the game decently now, but he was still struggling to actually play it.

Taylor was restless with anticipation again. Though, less so this time. He knew a lot of the other kids on the team, even if only in passing. He could at least guess at what position most of them would play.

It was no surprise when she announced Taylor was the starting pitcher for the first game. He often was. A girl named Jesed would be the reserve pitcher. Alyx announced several more positions before announcing Wil's.

Taylor looked over at Wil, who seemed restless and nervous.

Taylor didn't blame him a whit. As far as he was concerned, Wil was doing quite well given that he'd only been doing this for a week. But that didn't change the fact that their first game was tomorrow and Wil had to play somewhere.

A minute later they had an answer when Alyx listed Wil as one of the outfielders. Right field was a solid option. Wil shouldn't be too freaked out there.

They were headed back to the dugout to get their equipment when Wil sidled up to him. "Right fielder?" he asked, curiously.

"The outfielder on the right side of the field." Taylor clarified, pointing in the general direction of where Wil would play. "Babe Ruth was a right fielder," he shared. A random fun fact he didn't really expect Wil to care about but came to mind anyway.

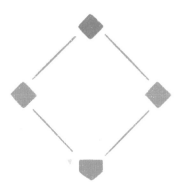

Wil

They played a couple of innings of a game that afternoon. Wil never managed to catch the ball when it came to him, but he did manage to throw it back to the infield a couple of times. He at least didn't feel like he was screwing anything up, which was simultaneously nice and a bit uncomfortable.

He had a sneaking suspicion that Alyx put him out here to get him out of the way, at least during these parts of the game. He had to bat some too. He could recognize that he was better than he had been at the beginning of the week.

Well, he was at least less likely to drop the bat outright. But he still never managed to actually hit the ball properly. The closest he came was a couple of sloppy hits that were immediately called foul. At least he wasn't the only one struggling though.

There were a couple of kids on the team who seemed nearly as inexperienced as he did, though both of them had at least played with friends before, even if that was it. Wil had tried to talk to them at one point during a break, but they clearly knew one another and he'd ended up backing away.

Too scared to try to introduce himself to new people and risk getting rejected and, entirely uncertain just what he might say, he headed back to Taylor instead, appreciative that he had at least a few people at camp that he did feel like he could talk to.

Taylor was sitting by himself, D20 flying from hand to hand in the way it seemed to whenever Taylor was restless. Wil settled down beside him on the bench, leaning against him for lack of a better backrest. Taylor shifted easily to accommodate his weight.

"So, first game tomorrow." Wil tried to open a conversation, feeling uncertain, but trying to hide his nerves.

Taylor nodded. "How do you feel?" he asked, and Wil shrugged in response.

"I don't know. Nervous. I'm glad I know what I'll be doing now, though."

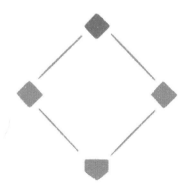

Taylor

Taylor's lips quirked up at that. He got the impression that Wil liked knowing the plan almost as much as he did, at least when it concerned him specifically. "You shouldn't have to worry too much," he tried to reassure. "Outfield's important, but it isn't likely to win or lose the game," he explained.

"And most batters are right-handed, so balls are more likely to go left field," he continued. "You shouldn't be kept too busy in the right field." Wil nodded, an expression settling on his face that Taylor couldn't read. He hoped that Wil was just processing.

"It's your first game ever." He smiled, wrapping an arm around Wil and pulling him in closer. "We ought to celebrate."

Wil grinned at that, the odd expression clearing from his face. "Yeah. I guess," he agreed readily enough.

Of course, the dinner in the dining hall was never going to be anything different than usual. They ate quickly, letting Jessie and Mateo's bickering over who would win their first match dominate the conversation. As they exited the dining hall, cones of soft-serve ice cream in hand, Taylor sought permission to loop an arm around Wil again.

"Well, what do you want to do tonight?" he asked cheerily, trying to keep his attention off of the game and on Wil right now. It was helpful to feel like Wil needed that too. Taylor could always redirect his thoughts better for someone else's sake than for his own.

"I don't know," he said. Taylor didn't blame him. They couldn't go anywhere by themselves. And most of the camp evening activities weren't that appealing. He and Wil bypassed them more evenings than not, typically both drained and ready to be done with people by the time dinner was finished.

"Can we just hang out and listen to music?" Wil asked after a moment of thought.

Taylor was always down for that. He wondered what Wil's taste in music was. "Sounds great," he agreed easily. "You DJ."

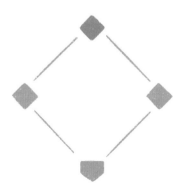

Wil

Wil pulled out his phone and debated what to play, though only for a moment. He listened to Taylor's baseball music; Taylor could deal with his show tunes, even if they weren't his favorite. Starting his favorite playlist, Wil plopped on the bed next to Taylor, finishing the last bite of his ice cream cone.

He realized a moment later that he shouldn't have assumed Taylor wouldn't like show tunes. He was happily singing along, belting out "Defying Gravity" in the most off-key ridiculously bad singing voice Wil had ever heard. Honestly, it was adorable.

Wil joined in, forgetting even attempting to match his voice with Taylor's and just throwing himself into the song. He'd always liked this one. Somewhere there was a video of him as a kindergartener singing it, all dressed up in every black piece of clothing he could find.

They'd danced to "For Good" at his ballet recital earlier that year and he'd been in love with the entire soundtrack ever since. Now, singing along to one of his favorite musicals with Taylor, he felt comfortable in a way he hadn't fully since the reality that he'd have to actually play baseball this summer had fully kicked in.

"You have an awful singing voice," he observed with a fond smile, before quickly second-guessing himself and backtracking. He didn't want to hurt Taylor's feelings.

But before he got an apology out he caught sight of Taylor's own amused expression. "I do," he agreed simply, with a chuckle.

"I still like singing with you," Wil said, instead of an apology.

Taylor smiled sweetly at that. "I'm glad." He took Wil's hand squeezing it. "I like singing with you too." And, Wil was trying really hard not to completely freak out at that. Taylor was holding his hand and complimenting him. What? "You're a really talented singer."

Wil missed Camp Fletcher fiercely and just being around theater in general. A scene like this, singing show tunes at the top of their lungs, happened all the time there. The only thing missing was the decorations, show posters and playbills, and cast photos on the walls.

Suddenly eager to hang all his decor, Wil hopped up and started extracting his suitcase from under the bed.

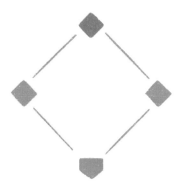

Taylor

Taylor watched bemusedly as Wil pulled a cardboard tube full of posters out of his suitcase and started doing his best to hang them up, straining to reach the tops of each one. He seemed to be considering how best to climb onto the desk when Taylor pushed himself up to join him.

"Hey, do you need help with that?" Taylor asked, well aware his height was an advantage at times like these.

"Yeah," Wil said, seeming appreciative but also a bit awkward. Taylor wondered why. He was perfectly used to helping out whenever a tall person was required. "If you can, that would be great."

They hung the posters together. Wil directed while Taylor got them into place, both of them still dancing around and singing along to Wil's playlist.

Taylor recognized a few show posters, but there were others he didn't. About three were signed. And there was a poster-sized, hand-drawn map labeled "Silverdell" in calligraphy at the top. "That's the setting for the campaign I'm running," Wil said when he saw Taylor looking.

"It's really cool," Taylor replied, wondering who had made it.

They finally finished, plopping down on the bed side by side again. "Thanks," said Wil, "and thanks for the help." He seemed to appreciate not having to do it on his own. And Taylor was glad that the room had more of Wil's interests on display now.

The song changed again to one that Taylor didn't recognize, but Wil clearly knew all the words. Wil seemed so happy just singing. If Taylor hadn't already known that he loved theater, it would be obvious now. Taylor was glad to see him finally relaxing somewhat. He'd seemed more and more stressed and anxious the past couple of days.

Wil still appeared a bit on edge again now though, a range of odd expressions flitting across his face. Taylor considered pulling away but dismissed the thought. Wil seemed to like being close as much as he did. That probably wouldn't be helpful. Instead, he just waited.

It took several minutes before Wil spoke again, songs still playing loudly while they waited. Taylor refrained from singing along this time though. Wil must have had a Broadway playlist. Taylor recognized more songs than not.

"Can I tell you something?" Wil said quietly, gripping Taylor's hand tightly. Taylor nodded his consent, curious what was going on. "I'm kind of worried that it'll mess up our friendship, and I don't want that." Wil started anxiously, rambling.

Taylor wished he could reassure him but knew he couldn't. So instead he simply sat and listened. "I also just want to be friends. I don't..." Wil trailed off, then started again. "I want to be honest about this, but I don't want it to change anything. It just feels weird not telling you. I don't know."

Taylor still didn't know what it was exactly that Wil wanted to tell him, so he didn't know how to respond. He liked Wil; he didn't think much would change that. But the reassurance wouldn't mean much without context.

"I like you," Wil said all in a rush, confusing Taylor. He liked him too. They were friends, weren't they? Wil had just said that, but he was already continuing. "I have a crush on you." Wil's cheeks were bright red, and he pressed his face into Taylor's arm a moment later.

Huh. Whatever Taylor had been expecting, it wasn't that. People their age got crushes? Really?

Wil

Wil kind of couldn't believe he had actually said that. But he was still pretty proud he had. Even if he was freaking out even more now. Taylor's arm was nice. It was soft and safe. Wil could just hide here forever, yeah?

Taylor hadn't actually replied yet. Maybe he was totally freaked out and uncomfortable. Though, if he was, he probably would have pulled away, right? Wil didn't know what to think. He mostly just wanted Taylor to say something, anything.

Instead, Taylor squeezed his hand again. The hand that he was still holding. Wil only realized then how tightly he'd been gripping it. He intentionally relaxed his fingers some, though he stayed where he was. He liked holding Taylor's hand.

"I don't know what to say," Taylor spoke after a long moment. Wil had kind of been expecting reassurance or upset or, he didn't know, some kind of emotional reaction. He pulled up again and looked at Taylor properly. Yeah. Taylor mostly just looked unsure of himself.

Well, that was fine. "You don't have to say anything in particular," Wil spoke quietly. "I really don't expect anything. I just wanted you to know." He didn't know why that had felt so important. He hadn't ever told a crush that he'd liked him before, but then again Wil hadn't been as close to any of his previous crushes as he was getting to Taylor.

"You're my friend. And I think you're really cute. I like you. It felt like something you should know." Wil felt oddly calm now, still a little bit off and slightly freaking out on the inside, but just because now Taylor knew. Not because he was worried. It was somehow really reassuring to realize that Taylor didn't know exactly how to navigate this stuff either.

"Thank you for sharing," Taylor said with an adorable smile, looking back at Wil. "Can I kiss your cheek?" he asked suddenly. And Wil blushed even brighter.

"Sure. That sounds nice," he forced himself to say, meaning every word of it.

Taylor dipped his head down and gave him a short simple kiss. Wil felt like he kind of melted a bit there.

Taylor

Taylor still didn't really know how to process any of this. It was all right that Wil liked him like that. He didn't think he felt the same way. But he trusted Wil not to be upset by that. It was all good. They were still friends. They could still be close.

Wil was really sweet and Taylor had wanted to kiss him. So he asked and Wil had agreed. Nothing had to change there. They could just keep navigating the friendship they were already building together.

Taylor was still just stuck on the idea that crushes were a thing. Sure, some of the guys he knew talked about their crush of the week, different girls they knew from school. But he'd never really taken it seriously.

That was all just pretending to be grown, right? He'd never really imagined that actual crushes were a thing. Not yet at least. But Wil was here and honest and his feelings seemed very real. Taylor didn't quite know what to do with that.

He wondered if it was normal to have crushes already. Or if Wil was ahead of the curve there? It seemed like poor timing to try to ask though, so he filed the thought away for further exploration. Taylor himself had never had a crush before.

He'd always assumed that was just typical, but maybe not? Maybe he was aromantic? Who knew? He certainly wasn't going to figure out the answer that evening. But it was an interesting thought. He'd seen the flag and looked it up, so he knew about aro people and all, but Taylor hadn't ever really considered before that he might be.

"You need anything?" he asked suddenly, realizing that Wil had leaned back into him at some point and fallen quiet for a while as well.

Wil sat up again at that, considering the question. "More music and singing?" he proposed with a happy expression.

Taylor chuckled. "The music hasn't gone anywhere," he observed, nodding towards Wil's phone. "Fair." Wil agreed, grabbing it and turning the music up. "More singing then." And that was it; he started singing along with the current song, getting up and dancing happily.

Taylor joined him, thoughts still swirling and glad of the distraction.

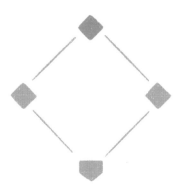

Wil

Wil was up late that evening. After Taylor went to sleep, he had to message Leila. *So, I may have told him I have a crush on him.* Her freaked-out responses were pretty fun. Wil teased out the information, enjoying watching his friend guess what happened.

He kissed me, he shared at one point, knowing exactly what reaction that would get but still thinking about that kiss himself though. He hadn't expected it. Sure, Taylor was pretty cuddly. But kisses, even cheek kisses, felt intimate to him in a way he hadn't expected. Not after sharing that. It seemed like a pretty clear sign that Taylor wasn't freaked out.

Wil didn't get the impression that it meant anything more than that either. He'd been pretty clear that he didn't want anything, not now. And, Taylor certainly hadn't suggested that he did. It was just... friendship. A different type of friendship than Wil had had before, though. It was nice.

Eventually, he did fill Leila in on the whole story. But only after keeping her guessing until late in the evening. Partially because he enjoyed the give and take of the conversation, had fun being the source of a bit of drama for once. But also because he didn't really know how to explain Taylor, how to describe his reactions or the easy platonic affection he shared so simply. He didn't know how to contrast that with Taylor's intense love of baseball, his fervent desire to win that Wil seemed to be the main thing standing in the way of.

Wil loved gossiping with Leila. And she happily filled him in on all of the theater camp shenanigans in return. Apparently, there were two new cute people and Leila couldn't decide which one she liked better. It was fun.

And Leila was happy for him. Proud of him for talking to Taylor and every bit as ridiculous as usual. He was enjoying himself so much that once he really got into the conversation he nearly forgot about the game.

Reminders of it hit him full force the next morning though. Even the teams that wouldn't be playing until tomorrow were excited, if only because it was the start of everything. Jessie and Mateo had made signs to cheer for them. It was actually really sweet.

But that aside, Wil was getting more and more nervous. Sure, right field may not be a crucial position, but would still be out there. And Taylor cared so much about this. Wil didn't want to let him down.

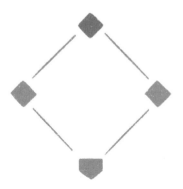

Taylor

Taylor had little time for thinking about crushes. His thoughts were entirely on the game. He spent much of the morning warming up, thinking about how it would feel to throw that first real pitch. His last game of the season hadn't been that long ago. But camp always felt different. New team, new experience.

He pulled out his D20, squeezed it tightly, and pulled it close to his face, only noticing Wil watching him a second later. "It's a good luck thing," he explained, tucking it into his pocket and pressing it safely down to the bottom.

"My Nanay had me roll it before one of the first games I pitched for." He smiled fondly at the memory. "I was really nervous and fidgeting with it like I do. She told me to roll it and I rolled a natural 20. We won the game. I've kept it on me during every game since."

Taylor tapped his pocket, feeling the comforting lump the die formed there, wished Wil luck and walked out towards the mound, leaving Wil to make his own way into the outfield. Taylor didn't know the catcher at all; this was his first year at camp. But that was fine. He watched for signals, getting the ball ready.

The game turned into a pitchers' duel. Their opponents had a good pitcher too. He and Taylor were probably some of the best players out there at the moment. The batters were doing all right, but they couldn't keep up. Taylor lost track of how many batters he struck out, getting into the rhythm of throwing pitch after pitch.

An advantage of having a designated hitter, beyond just not having to bat, was getting to watch more of the game from the dugout. His own team held their own at batting but weren't the best. Wil and the other new guys definitely weren't getting pitches that they stood a chance at. But that would change as they got more experience.

The game was pretty close most of the way through. The two teams were battling neck and neck. But their team managed to take the lead in the bottom of the sixth inning. Their opponents couldn't quite catch up, and Little League only played seven-inning games, so that was that. Game over.

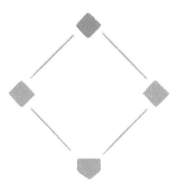

Wil

Well, of all the things Wil had worried about, getting bored out of his mind hadn't made the list. Apparently, it should have. He spent nearly half of the game standing out in his section of grass without a thing to do. Most people didn't even make it onto base. And any time they did hit the ball, it always went towards the other half of the field.

Wil got the most opportunity to move running in and out from the outfield when the teams switched sides. If he was bored in the outfield, he was lousy at batting. He kept striking out. He'd think he had it and ought to swing and then miss. Or that there was no way and stay put and the umpire would call a strike.

Then he got pulled out halfway through. One of the new kids he'd been scared to introduce himself to before got put in right field in his place. Wil would wonder what he'd done wrong to get removed, but he knew that the real issue was he hadn't done anything at all.

They won, and Wil knew he ought to be happy about that. But he still wished that he'd contributed in some way, even if it wasn't much. Meanwhile, Taylor was the hero of the game. He'd pitched so well few players had even made it to first. As a result, Taylor was practically surrounded the moment the game was over. Everyone was cheering and clapping him on the back.

Wil wondered for a moment how Taylor was handling being surrounded like that. And the noise. How was everyone that loud? But he supposed Taylor was probably used to it. Champion player and all that. Wil settled onto the bench in the dugout and waited for the excitement to pass.

Wil knew that he probably would have been relieved if someone had told him this was an option before camp. That he could basically do nothing and it wouldn't matter. He would have jumped at the chance to stay out of the action.

But now he couldn't shake the feeling of disappointment. He understood baseball now. Even if he didn't love it, he still wished that he could really feel like a part of it. That since he and Taylor were on the same team, he could at least feel like that mattered.

It was hard feeling like he'd been stuck in the outfield and ignored. And even harder watching all of the attention Taylor got. Well deserved. Even Wil could see that he was a talented player. But, still, it just meant that he kept on being ignored. Even after the game was over.

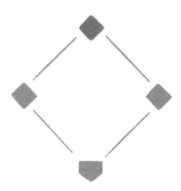

Taylor

Taylor finally shook off the crowd. He got the excitement. He really did. He was pretty ecstatic himself. But he still hated being surrounded like that. He'd rather celebrate on his own. Or at least with just his closest friends.

Looking around he caught sight of Wil. It seemed like he'd gotten a bit sunburned. Baseball would do that to you. Taylor made a mental note to share his sunscreen next time. He made his way over, snagging his water bottle from where it sat next to Wil's and draining what was left in it.

"Good game," he remarked with a contented smile.

"Congrats," Wil offered, and Taylor's grin stretched wider.

"Thanks." Taylor really was pleased. That was some of the best pitching he'd done in a while. That proud happy feeling stayed with him through the rest of the afternoon and into dinner. But by the time they got out of an after-dinner game night he was starting to worry about Wil.

It seemed like he was feigning normalcy, but Taylor had caught that odd expression on his face more than once. And he'd gotten quieter and quieter as the evening wore on. Even at the board game night, which Taylor had expected to be right up his alley. He wondered what was going on.

He would have expected Wil to feel better now that they were through the first game. And since they'd won. But Wil almost seemed to be worse off now than he was before the game.

Once they were back in their dorm, Taylor turned to him almost immediately. "Everything all right, Wil?" he asked, looking concerned. Something was clearly wrong, but Taylor had no idea what.

"Yeah. I'm fine." Wil managed. "I just miss Camp Fletcher," he said, looking away from Taylor. He turned to the wall of show posters, and then picked up a framed photo of a group of people on stage. "My theater camp. That was my place," he continued, "Somewhere I felt comfortable and talented and completely at home. I think it's the same kind of place for me that this camp is for you."

Taylor's gaze followed Wil's. Wil did look confident in that photo. He was center stage, in a glittery costume, arms held high in the air. Taylor could easily imagine what it must be like to see him perform. All confidence and flamboyance. Wil's last statement was a sobering one. Taylor hadn't really processed how much Wil was missing out on by being here.

Taylor knew that he would be devastated if he had to miss Sluggers. He looked forward to this month all year. It explained how off Wil had seemed at various points over the past few days. Especially because he'd never be able to shine at baseball the same way he did on stage.

An idea started to churn into being at that thought, but he didn't want to say anything yet. He'd hate to get Wil's hopes up for nothing. "That's valid. It's okay for it to be hard," he offered instead, wrapping Wil into a solid side hug the moment he got a nod of assent to do so.

He was up again for way longer than he ought to be that evening. Taylor had always been that way. Any time he had a problem to solve or an idea in mind, he couldn't stop thinking about it. He was gradually learning that not everyone wanted him to swoop in and try to fix all of their problems, but it was admittedly a work in progress.

He hoped that Wil didn't think he was being overbearing this time. He really did just want to recreate some part of what he was missing. Taylor knew he couldn't bring all of his friends to camp, couldn't fix everything. But maybe he could at least give

Wil a moment in the spotlight.

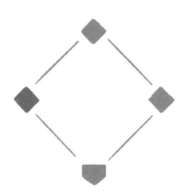

Part Three

Wil

Wil was startled to realize Taylor was gone the next morning. Taylor typically seemed to wake up before him, but this was the first time he'd actually gone anywhere. It shouldn't have worried Wil as much as it did. They'd only roomed together for a week. It wasn't like he could honestly claim to know Taylor's usual routines.

He probably just went to breakfast early for once. Maybe with Jessie and Mateo. He probably didn't want to hang out with Wil anymore. And there it was. All the anxiety he'd tried to push away rushing in and explaining everything.

Wil hadn't done a thing the whole game. All Taylor's hard work coaching him, trying to help him, had been for naught. He'd been put way out in the middle of nowhere where he couldn't affect a thing. No doubt Taylor was disappointed.

And he'd made things weird. You didn't just tell your roommate you had a crush on them. Who did that? Taylor was probably so focused on the game yesterday he mostly forgot about it, but now... Of course, he wanted some space.

Wil was aware he was probably overblowing things. He knew logically that Taylor had reacted well when they'd talked. Heck, he'd asked to kiss Wil's cheek. That wasn't something he would have done if he was uncomfortable, right?

And Wil hadn't really messed the game up; he just hadn't done anything. It wasn't great, but they'd still won. So, there was no real reason for Taylor to be upset about that. Goodness knew, all that time Taylor spent coaching him apparently hadn't taken away from his own ability to win. It had been quite clear Taylor was the star of that match.

Still, knowing logically that things probably weren't as dire as his anxiety made them out to be didn't actually help with the anxiety. Wil needed to distract himself. He considered messaging Leila, but it was 9:00 on a Sunday morning, and she'd no doubt be at church.

He ended up scrolling aimlessly on his phone for a while, hopping from one app to another, none of them really holding his attention. He needed to talk to someone. It was convenient that an additional voicemail notification buzzed up at that point.

His dad had called last night after the game, but Wil had been too out of it and disappointed to respond then. He could call his dad now though. Get a fresh perspective and maybe some reassurance. That would be nice.

Taylor

"A talent show?" Coach Rose still seemed somewhat surprised. She was always in whatever conference room they'd turned into an office for her this time of the morning, but Taylor didn't get the impression she saw a lot of campers during that time.

"Well, a variety show actually," he clarified. "But, yes, same general concept. I just don't want the name to make anyone think they have to be particularly talented." Taylor tried to explain the slight nuance. "I'm not imagining anything major, just something fun for the end of camp. People can do whatever they enjoy and it'll be fun to watch even for folks who don't perform."

Coach Rose was smiling slightly now, that fond, slightly amused smile she often seemed to have. "And I suppose your friend, Wil, might like to perform?" she asked knowingly.

Taylor was momentarily caught off guard but recovered quickly. "I hope so," he shared honestly. "I think so."

Coach Rose waited silently, head tilted slightly. Taylor was perfectly comfortable in the silence, simply sitting patiently. After a long moment, she nodded sharply. "I have no issues with it, but you'll need to do the bulk of the planning. Can you handle that?" she asked seriously.

Taylor took a moment to consider. He wasn't completely inexperienced at putting on events of this nature. He had certainly been roped into half stage-managing his moms' drag shows more than once before. But he hadn't ever done anything like this completely by himself before.

His mind was already swirling through everything that would need to happen. They'd need a space. And someone to handle the music. And sign-ups. Probably a rehearsal time. It would be a lot. It took him a long moment to remember that he did not need to do everything alone.

"I think I can get a group together to plan it," he said thoughtfully. "If you're tentatively approving it, I can draw up a plan before we make an announcement?" Taylor proposed. He couldn't imagine Wil and Jessie and Mateo being unwilling to help, but he wouldn't want to commit them to anything without asking first.

Coach Rose nodded again, smiling warmly. "Sounds very sensible," she agreed. "I'll expect a plan from you by tomorrow morning." Taylor nodded his agreement. He could do that. They'd have to work quickly to have everything together by the end of camp, but he had faith they could pull it off.

He just couldn't wait to tell Wil.

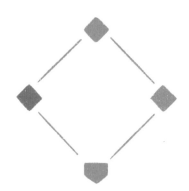

Wil

"Congratulations!" His dad sounded overjoyed when Wil had said they'd won, his voice filled with obvious pride. Wil had to swallow down a fresh bout of anxiety. His dad didn't know he hadn't actually done anything to be proud of. It was hard feeling like he was about to disappoint him.

"Dad?" he interrupted tentatively, getting his dad's attention immediately.

"Yes, son?" he asked, bringing an immediate feeling of warmth. His dad might not really get anything, but goodness he was trying. Wil still really loved it when he called him "son."

That made him feel better about sharing what was going on, tough as it was. "We won." He reiterated the initial statement that had made his dad so pleased. "But I didn't really do anything," he continued after a breath. "I was in the outfield. The ball barely even came to me."

Wil knew that technically wasn't anything that he had control over, but it still didn't make it any easier. Plus, the whole reason he was put out there was so he didn't mess up anything. He felt ashamed admitting that to his father, but it was mostly the reason he'd called in the first place.

"They put me in right field because I'm not any good. I've been trying so hard." His voice broke and he initially fought back his tears before giving in and letting them fall. Taylor cried, there was no reason he couldn't too. "Honestly, I never really cared about baseball. I'm sorry, Dad. I just don't."

His dad murmured a bit of reassurance, but Wil kept going. "I still want to do well though. Or, at least, all right. I want you to be proud of me." Wil hadn't realized how important that was until the words were out, but there was no denying it now.

His dad drew in a long breath, leaving Wil anxious and uncertain while he waited for a response. He needn't have worried though. "Oh, kiddo. Wil," his dad started. "I am always so proud of you." Wil could hear the weight behind the words.

"You are a good-hearted, talented kid. And you are growing into a wonderful young man." Wil smiled through his tears, not really certain how to respond to that but feeling really touched and happy.

"Thanks, Dad," he managed. "I love you so much."

For all that he sometimes felt out of place or distanced from his dad, there were also moments that reminded Wil just how much he cared. And that was worth so much. Still, he had to ask. "You wouldn't like me better if I was the kind of guy who's into baseball and all that?"

It was the kind of irksome anxiety that he knew full well was just anxiety. Wil was perfectly aware of how much his dad loved him. And, yet...

His dad simply scoffed in response. "What hobbies you do or don't enjoy couldn't make a bit of difference in how much I love you, kiddo," he reassured.

"I'm sorry if I pressured you into camp," he continued, sounding anxious now himself. "I didn't mean to. Just, after you came out, I really wanted you to know how much I support you. And that seemed like a good way. I guess I didn't really think it through." He ended bashfully.

Wil could practically picture his expression and could easily imagine how he felt. Yeah. There were some ways in which he absolutely took after his dad. "It's all right," he promised. "I don't think I'll ever want to do it again. But it's actually been kind of cool. I like that I'm learning about something that's really important to you."

Wil had already learned so much more about his dad in the past week. Superficial things like what position he'd played. But more important things too; Wil was learning that he could be part of building a more active relationship with him. And that was pretty awesome.

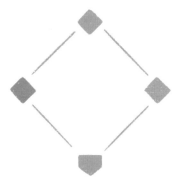

Taylor

Taylor looped Jessie and Mateo in first, banging on their door until a sleepy-looking Mateo finally let him in. Jessie didn't waste a moment, already glaring at him from the top bunk. "We only get two days to sleep in!" she growled, annoyed.

"I know. I know. I'm sorry." Actually, Taylor hadn't considered that at first. It was still early. He tended to forget about that kind of thing. But now he was here, so there was no changing it. "I'm sorry!" he repeated, shying away from Jessie's baleful glare.

"I'll get you breakfast after this?" he offered with what he hoped was a puppy dog expression. There ought to be time to get to the dining hall still.

That won her over. "Fine. I'll give in to your bribery," she conceded with a sigh, but he knew she loved him.

"Hey, you woke me up too." Mateo protested, with an exaggerated yawn. "Don't I get breakfast?"

Taylor chuckled. "Yes, yes, breakfast all around," he promised. "I hope you like take-out containers full of cereal."

"Always." Jessie agreed cheerfully, already getting back to her usual energy. "Now, what was so important?" she asked, leaping down from the bed and landing perfectly. She looped an arm around Mateo and turned them both to face Taylor.

Taylor laid out his whole plan for them. Explaining the why before starting to go into all of the little details. "I want Wil to have a way to shine," he found himself sharing. "But not just him. Everyone. Or to try something new. Just a space that people can do the things that make them happy." He was falling even more in love with the idea himself. And not just for Wil's sake. He thought it could be a good thing for a lot of people.

Jessie and Mateo were both nodding. "I could do a stand-up routine!" Mateo proposed excitedly.

"I'm getting pretty good at juggling," Jessie added.

Taylor grinned at them. "I can't wait to see." He meant it. It would be a blast to see all of his friends perform. "So, you'll help me plan it?" he confirmed. It took a bit more discussion of everything that would need to happen for both his friends to agree.

"Hey, didn't you promise us cereal?" Jessie chimed in with a playful nudge once they'd started to come to an end of the discussion.

"Yes, fine, I see what this is about." Taylor played like he was put out, but he didn't really mind. He liked feeding his loved ones. He got it from his Nanay.

He was in and out of the dining hall in under ten minutes, leaving with several take-out containers full of cereal balanced precariously on top of one another. Stabilizing them with his chin, he carefully made his way back to the dorms.

"Cereal," he called out cheerfully at their door and Mateo let him in. It was nice, hanging out with two of his best friends. Sometimes it felt so unfair that they lived as far away as they did. Taylor tried to savor these moments when they did happen.

"Hey, question." He spoke out of the blue, interrupting Jessie and Mateo's scuffle for the container of Froot Loops. They both looked over, took in his expression, shrugged, and seemingly came to a mutual unspoken agreement to share the cereal.

Taylor felt a bit weird now that Jessie and Mateo were both looking at him. "So, do you get crushes?" He asked awkwardly, running a hand through his hair. "Not on anyone specific. Or like, I guess it's cool if you do, but just in general?" He tried to clarify, well aware he was probably just making his question even more confusing.

"Yeah. Of course, I do," Mateo replied with a grin and a shrug. "There's this one boy on my Little League team, Esteban, I've told you about him?" He trailed off, smiling.

"You seriously didn't pick up on this?" Jessie asked Taylor with a laugh. "Mateo's only been pining over him for like a year now."

"Weird. I mean, not weird, sorry. Just new." Taylor stumbled over his words. "That's cool. You should totally talk to him. Just... crushes? I kind of thought we didn't really get them yet? I haven't." He shrugged.

Jessie looked thoughtful. "Fair enough. Some people might not. I do too, though. I think a lot of people do from what I've seen."

Taylor nodded and let the conversation move on. Neither of his friends pressed him on it, chatting happily about Esteban who Taylor had definitely heard lots about but hadn't realized Mateo liked like that. This whole crush business still seemed kind of fake, but he trusted his friends. So, aro, maybe? Huh.

Noticing the time, Taylor realized Wil would probably be up by now. "I'm gonna go." He extricated himself from the conversation, eager to tell Wil about the variety show. He would be so surprised.

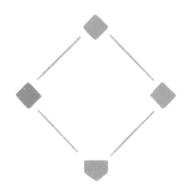

Wil

"A talent show?"

Taylor's eyes sparkled with something that looked like amusement. "A variety show," he clarified. Wil didn't really see the difference. Either way, that seemed like something totally out of place for baseball camp.

"Yeah. It's not a normal thing we do, but Coach Rose approved and Jessie and Mateo are going to help," Taylor explained passionately, hands flapping wildly. He was obviously delighted. And, apparently, he'd talked to a lot of people already.

"Sounds like fun." Wil agreed. Normally it's the type of thing he would have loved. He still didn't entirely know what to make of it in this context though. It wasn't something he'd expected. Taylor had definitely managed to take him by surprise.

He listened attentively as Taylor discussed everything he was imagining. Wil was a bit taken aback by just how much theater experience he seemed to have, but he supposed it made sense when he thought about it. Taylor definitely had a good plan.

"So, what do you think?" Taylor stopped suddenly, turning right toward Wil. He sounded inquisitive, but also a bit uncertain. It seemed like he really wanted Wil's approval, wanted Wil to be pleased. That as much as anything made Wil's heart melt.

"I love it." He grinned, fond and exuberant and feeling totally happy at camp for once. "Thank you. It's going to be amazing." Wil knew it would be a bit thrown together. But, really, what performance wasn't? It would be cool to see what everyone chose to do for it.

"So, you'll help me plan it?" Taylor asked explicitly. Wil nodded his agreement, already thinking about everything that needed to happen. Taylor had a good plan, but it would still be a lot of work.

"And I have to decide what to perform," Wil realized with delight.

He loved putting together performances. That was his favorite part of theater camp every year. He loved all of the little details. Planning costumes and choreography and picking music. Seeing a performance come together, piece by piece, rehearsal by rehearsal was always so cool.

Taylor was grinning at him and, goodness, how was he that pretty? "I can't wait to see it," he said earnestly and Wil blushed.

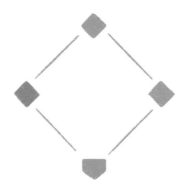

Taylor

They had an unusually quiet lunch for once. Taylor always found that amusing. As fiercely, lovingly competitive as Jessie and Mateo were, any time they had an actual game coming up between them they tended to fall silent.

He knew that camp was one of the only places that they played on different teams. They'd been on the same Little League team since they were eight. He and Mateo had talked a lot at the beginning of last year when Jessie started middle school. It had been hard for both of them to be split up.

After the game, they'd no doubt be back to their usual selves, teasing one another incessantly about everything that happened during it. But now they each ate silently, leaving Taylor and Wil responsible for leading the conversation.

Taylor declined that particular responsibility, and Wil appeared to as well, leaving the entire group oddly quiet. Taylor was looking forward to the game this afternoon. He loved getting to watch baseball almost as much as he liked playing. He knew at least half of the campers fairly well, which always made it more fun.

He hoped that Wil enjoyed it too. He knew that his moms were inevitably really bored by the end of a baseball game, for all that they humored him. His Nanay had remarked once that three hours was such a *long* span of time. Taylor had noted in return that they had been known to have D&D sessions that lasted twice that.

"How are you feeling about the game?" he asked toward the end of the meal, feeling an obligation to strike up at least a bit of conversation. Jessie came alert at that. "I have no doubt we're going to win," she asserted.

Mateo stuck his tongue out at her. "We'll see."

With that both of them were chuckling, Taylor and Wil joining in. "Good game," Mateo told Jessie with a broad smile.

"You too," she agreed, jostling him slightly.

Taylor grinned. "I'm cheering for both of you."

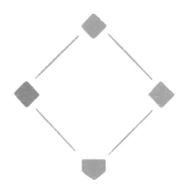

Wil

Taylor insisted on swinging by their room before the game. Wil followed along, always happy to stick together. Apparently, Taylor had to get his scorebook. Given that it clearly wasn't Taylor's responsibility to score the game, Wil was curious but generally in support.

As it turned out, a scorebook was exactly what it sounded like. Taylor just wanted to keep his own record of the score and everything that happened in the game. "Why?" Wil asked curiously, uncertain what the appeal of doing so might be.

"It's fun. I like seeing the numbers and patterns and whatnot at the end of the game," Taylor said. "Like, how did different batters do compared to one another. Or if there was a big shift associated with a pitching change." Wil doubted he'd ever stop being surprised by just how many baseball terms he understood now.

"It also gives me something to do with my hands." Taylor continued his explanation, fingers tapping demonstratively against his palm. "I've always needed something to do while I watch things, some kind of stim or activity of whatnot." Wil nodded. Yeah, he'd definitely noticed that.

The game started off a lot more dramatically than theirs had the previous day. The score was already 7-9 by the third inning. Wil was pretty positive they'd still been 0-0 at that point in their own game. Runners were actually making it on base this time.

Wil continued to be startled by the realization that he actually followed what was happening. There were a few little details he clarified with Taylor, but most of it made sense. It really was easier to think of it all in D&D terms, but it also felt like he was getting confident with baseball outside of that framework.

In retrospect, he thought his anxiety about being expected to know anything about the game had played as big a role in his lack of understanding as the actual complexity of baseball. Taylor had helped him get out of his fears and start thinking of it the same way he could any other game he was learning. Well, like any other game, but with the addition of an obnoxious amount of running and flying balls coming at his head.

"Wait? I think Mateo's trying to..." Wil started, noticing an odd bit of movement. Mateo was further off base than he'd expect, and it kind of looked like he was getting ready to run.

"Hmm?" Taylor replied curiously, following his gaze.

"He's stealing," Wil exclaimed just as Mateo broke into a full run.

"Yeah!" Taylor laughed delightedly, on the edge of his seat as he watched the drama. The pitcher tried to respond and get the ball back in time but didn't manage it.

"He's safe now, right?" Wil confirmed as Mateo slid into second.

Taylor nodded, clapping wildly. "Yep. He's safe." He sounded proud. "The catcher didn't notice until it was too late," Taylor explained.

Wil scrutinized the field. "It's the catcher's job to spot things like that, 'cause the pitcher can't see?"

"That's right," Taylor agreed, excitement fading as the game fell back into the typical rhythm of play. "You would have caught him," he remarked, eyes still on the game. Wil was surprised by that. It felt odd to be told he could have managed something that the other players hadn't, and yet Taylor sounded pretty certain of it.

"Catcher!" he exclaimed. "It's perfect." Wil was listening but looked a bit confused. Taylor wasn't confident that he was following, so he backtracked accordingly. "You could play catcher," he explained, trying to actually connect his thoughts out loud. He knew he had a habit of jumping from one idea to the next without any explanation.

"You have a good eye for the game. And that's crucial for a catcher. You need to be able to keep track of everything happening on the field and signal accordingly." Taylor explained.

"You think I can do that?" Wil retorted with a raised eyebrow, and even Taylor couldn't miss the disbelief in his tone.

"You did this afternoon," he stated plainly. Wil had caught that Mateo was trying to steal before seemingly anyone else had.

"Maybe, once." Wil acknowledged, still seeming resistant. "But I wasn't actually playing then. It's easier just watching."

"Hmm. Why's that?" Taylor inquired, curious.

Wil took time to ponder before answering. "I'm so much more on edge while I play. And it feels like I have to keep up with everything," he said thoughtfully. Taylor nodded, that made sense. "Plus, I was really just watching Mateo then. He was the only kid out there that I knew," Wil added. "So, of course, I noticed him trying to steal."

Taylor shrugged in response to that. "I was watching him too and I didn't catch it," he shared honestly.

Wil gave him an odd look back but otherwise ignored it. "I thought Alyx made me an outfielder, so I couldn't mess things up," he said, staring determinedly down at that ground.

"Maybe," Taylor acknowledged. "But that doesn't mean she can't mix things up before the next game." He tried to reassure him. That was part of the point of camp, letting folks figure out what they were good at.

Wil still appeared less than convinced, so Taylor continued. "Hey, wanna just give it a try?" he suggested with what he hoped was a comforting smile. "We don't actually choose our positions after all. You can just practice some and then see what happens."

Wil got another odd expression at that, still looking down. But he nodded. "All right. I'll try," he agreed, leaving Taylor still feeling a bit uneasy. He didn't want to pressure Wil into anything, but he wasn't certain how to read his expression. And something made him hesitant to ask outright what was going on.

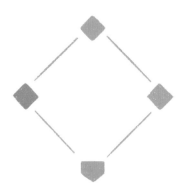

Wil

The variety show was one thing. Now this as well. Catcher? That was one of the key positions, wasn't it? Especially the way that Taylor had explained it. Strategy? Reading the game? Wil couldn't do things like that. It felt...

Wil shrugged to himself. It felt almost patronizing. Like Taylor was taking pity on him. Which, honestly, was something he was way too used to. People realized how anxious he was and started jumping in to make it easy. Not trusting him to do things well and feeling too bad for him to let him fail.

It wasn't entirely surprising from Taylor. One thing Wil had certainly learned about him was how incredibly nice he was. Always so supportive. He wanted Wil to feel good about himself, even if there was no real reason to.

Wil struggled with that. He wanted to impress Taylor. Wanted to make him proud in the same way that Taylor had so obviously been proud of Mateo. The way Taylor was proud of all of his friends. But this wasn't his element. And Taylor knew that, so he was doing this instead.

Wil wanted to resent it, but he couldn't. It just hurt instead. He'd been so excited about the concept of a variety show. Surprised, of course. But genuinely thrilled. And honestly, he still was. That at least was something he knew he could do well at. Even if the only reason Taylor was planning it was because there was no chance Wil could be even halfway decent at baseball.

Now that he'd realized what was really going on though, it felt a bit... tainted. It was hard to feel like he needed something special just for him. Just so he could feel good about himself. Wil fought with those feelings, beginning to wonder why Taylor bothered so much with him at all.

Did Taylor actually enjoy his company, or was he just too nice to let Wil flounder by himself? The latter was starting to feel more and more likely. And that was the worst feeling of all.

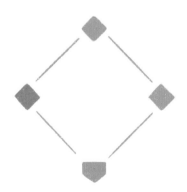

Taylor

The variety show planning was going well. They'd found a space. And Jessie had a great plan worked up to promote it. They already had about a dozen people signed up. It was nice to feel like it was really coming together.

"Stage, performers, tech, posters, what else?" Taylor thought aloud.

"Costumes!" Wil contributed almost immediately.

"That's the best part of any show." Mateo nodded his agreement.

"Where on earth are we supposed to get costumes?" Jessie asked, always practical. "This is baseball camp. Most kids just pack jeans and t-shirts." Then it was Taylor's turn to nod, she had a point. Costumes weren't going to be easy to come by here.

"We could make them?" Wil proposed tentatively.

"Out of what?" Mateo sounded curious. Taylor knew that tone. He wasn't opposed to the idea, just considering it. The two tossed ideas back and forth for a bit, but Taylor had his own idea percolating in his head.

"I could ask my moms." He spoke up after Wil and Mateo had fallen silent, not wanting to interrupt their conversation. "We have a bunch of fun costume stuff. Tutus and boas and make-up. That kind of thing. And I know our friends have a lot more."

"That would be awesome!" Mateo exclaimed. Taylor smiled. Mateo always got excited about the prospect of fun clothes.

"I can call them later today and ask if they'll bring things up on family weekend," he proposed, already feeling confident about the plan. His moms' drag wardrobe took more space than their day-to-day clothes. Anything they were good with loaning would be perfect.

"Do you think that's really the kind of costume things we need?" Wil sounded hesitant. Taylor turned to face him, confused.

"What do you mean?"

"Just, it's mostly guys here and the things you described... well they're kind of girly, aren't they?"

Huh. Now Taylor understood. He started to respond, but Jessie beat him to it. "Why should that matter?" she argued, hands on her hips.

Wil simply shrugged. "It shouldn't, I guess. But, does that really mean it doesn't? I mean, it's not like this is theater camp. All these guys came here for sports. Do we really expect them to be suddenly into glitter and everything?"

"I am," Taylor said frankly, eliciting more surprise from Wil than he would have expected.

"Seriously?" Wil asked, voice filled with disbelief.

"Eh. Not every day. Tulle is pretty scratchy. And, don't even get me started on lace. It's a sensory nightmare." Taylor shrugged. "But, yeah, I don't have anything against glitter. Or anything else 'girly' for that matter." He made air quotes around the word girly. Wil still looked dubious, but less sure of himself.

"He looks pretty in a flower crown," Mateo tossed in with a smile.

"It's true," Taylor confirmed. "I have photos." He pulled his phone out and started scrolling through it. Ma reposted wedding pictures at least a couple of times each year, so they should be easy enough to find. "That was me at my moms' wedding," he explained, showing off the photo once he found a good one.

Wil

"Aww. You were adorable." Wil leaned in to look closer. "You didn't feel weird or anything?" he asked, glancing back up to Taylor as he said it. Sure, Taylor wasn't quite like other guys Wil had known, but he still seemed so... just so much like what everyone expected. Wil never would have guessed he wore flower crowns.

"No, I like flower crowns. They're a bit of a family tradition," Taylor shared, swiping to another photo that showed him with his moms, all sporting colorful flower crowns. It was sweet. Taylor looked about five or six years old, curls longer than they were now, the same serious expression Wil had seen more than once before on his face.

It was also different from anything Wil had seen before. He'd always kind of assumed that being a boy meant he had to give up some of the things he liked. Sure, he was gay and pretty flamboyant. He was never going to be the kind of guy his dad was, but still...

It was weird. Taylor wore jeans and a t-shirt every day and coached him in baseball. He played sports and read graphic novels and listened to hip hop. Sure, he knew musical soundtracks as well. But Wil knew full well that no one would question Taylor's gender, not in the least.

At least, not normally maybe? Because apparently he liked flower crowns and it sounded like it was more than that. Wil was almost embarrassed to realize how much he hadn't considered that being an option. He'd kind of thought you were normal or you weren't. That boys who liked theater and glitter always stood out. But here was a photo of little Taylor in a flower crown and a dress, looking perfectly content. And that's something Wil never would have guessed about him. It was nice.

"That's cool," he managed after a bit, not certain how to put all of his thoughts and feelings into words. Not sure that he even wanted to try. "I didn't realize. But, that's really cool." Wil felt so awkward. "You were adorable there." He tried to make himself sound normal. And little Taylor really had been cute.

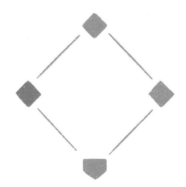

Taylor

Taylor felt weird walking back to their dorm room together. He was usually pretty comfortable with who he was. But conversations like that made it hard. He hadn't expected that from Wil. For him to be so surprised and odd about Taylor wearing flowers or whatever. And sure he'd gotten over it, but still...

Sometimes he felt so pulled between two worlds. When he was in his moms' world, he stood out because he liked baseball and usually just wore whatever was at the top of his dresser. Honestly, who has the mental energy to plan whole outfits every time they get dressed? Taylor didn't know how Mateo did it.

But here and at school and during baseball practice, all of a sudden he was weird because he liked flowers and dresses. Which, seriously? Dresses were the best. You didn't have to deal with waistbands pressing into you and you got to twirl. Taylor loved the feeling of fabric swinging around his legs. If more dresses had pockets and didn't tear so easily whenever he played sports, he'd wear them way more often.

It's just ... Taylor didn't feel all that different when he was on his own. But as soon as you put him with other people that changed. And it was extra hard getting it from Wil, because he didn't expect that from him. A trans guy at baseball camp? Taylor had been thrilled.

Even when it turned out that Wil wasn't really all that into baseball. It was still nice to feel like his two worlds were getting at least a little bit closer. Now he didn't know what to make of it. He found himself restless as ever that evening, pacing the room, fingers tapping steadily.

Eventually, he left so that he could pace the halls instead, die flying back and forth between his hands, full of pent-up energy and not enough places to send it. He wished he had someone to talk to about this stuff. Someone who could understand.

It was convenient his Ma called because, honestly, Taylor had never even considered talking to her about this kind of thing. Why would she know anything about it? But the moment he explained, she simply laughed. "Taylor, sweetie, I'm a nerdy 6'2" trans woman. No, I'll never know exactly what you're going through, love. But, I do know something about feeling out of place and judged for liking more traditionally feminine things."

Which, yeah, Taylor had to admit that she had a point. He just hadn't thought of it before. She was his Ma. Not exactly the first person he thought to come to for advice about being a guy. "Taylor, you are an awesome human. And I have no doubt your people are out there. Even if they are a bit hard to find now." His Ma spoke with all the passion she brought to city council meetings or D&D sessions.

"Sure. Not everyone will understand you. But that's on them, not you." Taylor smiled. He did know that. He tried to explain why it was extra hard with Wil. "Sweetie, stop a moment." His Ma paused him when he started to repeat himself. "It sounds to me like Wil is the kind of kid you get on well with. But he's also probably still figuring out a lot himself.

"You said he only just came out?" Taylor nodded, forgetting his Ma couldn't see the gesture over the phone. But she continued anyway, used to his lengthy silences. "Think about it from his perspective." Not really his strong suit, but Taylor tried. "He's probably still getting used to what being a boy means for him. Do you think he actually intended to hurt you?"

Taylor took a moment to think about it. To consider the question taking into account everything he knew about Wil so far. "No, I don't think so," he finally concluded.

"Okay, then," Ma replied. "It doesn't change the fact that he did hurt you or mean that you can't be impacted by that, but it may help you figure out what to do now."

"Yeah. That makes sense." Taylor had a lot more to think about, but that had helped. "Thanks, Ma."

"Any time, sweetie. I love you, pumpkin."

"Love you too, Ma."

Wil

Wil kind of wished Taylor hadn't left. Though he understood why. These little rooms were certainly not made for pacing. And Taylor seemed to need to move a lot. Wil, on the other hand, found himself curled into a tight ball, taking up as little space as possible.

He hated how jealous he was of Taylor. Wil loved his dad. He always had. But, wow, seeing photos of Taylor's family. The flower crowns and dresses. The way his moms' held him. Wil couldn't help but wish he'd had that. The chance to be a boy and still be exactly who he wanted to be. His dad tried. But, heck, his idea of how to support a son was by sending him to baseball camp. And that was the last thing Wil actually wanted.

When Taylor came back, looking thoughtful but stiller than he had been, fingers just rubbing his D20 instead of flying rapidly, Wil couldn't help but share. Taylor was someone he could trust with all of his complex messy feelings.

"Dad loves me. He loves me a lot, but..." Wil found himself trying to explain. He felt guilty saying this, though he didn't think Taylor would judge him. Taylor was watching him without much expression, but Wil chalked it up to him being tired. He'd noticed that facial expressions required effort for Taylor.

"We don't have a lot in common. And he doesn't really understand me. It's hard sometimes. He tries and I appreciate it, but he never really gets it right." Wil finished, still feeling unsure of how to explain. The words had come quickly once he finally started, but then they came to a crashing halt. His theater friends got this kind of thing. He didn't know if Taylor would.

Taylor just listened quietly, his expression still completely neutral. But when Wil held the silence he raised his arm and asked permission to touch in the way that Wil was beginning to expect from him. A simple wordless way of offering physical contact.

Wil nodded consent and Taylor's arm settled heavily across his shoulder. It was odd to think that his size had seemed intimidating when they first met. Taylor was tall and sturdy and Wil appreciated that about him now. He felt safe with him.

"Family can be complex," Taylor said simply. He related to a lot of what Wil was saying. And, that helped him understand so much better where Wil had been coming from earlier. It was tricky. "I feel the same way a lot of the time," he shared, noting how Wil reacted to that. He seemed almost startled. Taylor wondered why.

"My moms are great, but ninety percent of our interests are completely opposite," he found himself explaining, his hurt feelings already dissipating. No one knew where he got his love of sports from. He used to get signed up for a different YMCA camp every week during summer when he was little because both his parents worked and that had been the start of it.

"I attended a week-long sports camp and fell in love," he reminisced. "But it's not just sports. I don't know." He had a hard time defining it. "I'm different from my parents. I suppose most people are," Taylor mused.

Wil leaned further against him. "Yeah, I guess so." He sounded discontent. "It seems weird to me that you have that disconnect with your parents because they seem like they'd understand me so easily," Wil continued. Taylor got the sense he was thinking aloud. "I thought once that my dad would have preferred a son like you though," he confessed.

Taylor simply squeezed him, uncertain what to say. It felt like the type of statement he ought to debate, but he knew better than that. He'd never met Wil's dad, didn't know what kind of person he was. And he knew full well that some parents didn't deserve to be defended.

"He wouldn't actually want that." Wil seemed to realize where he'd left the conversation hanging. "I do think he'd like you though."

Taylor smiled at that, glad to hear that Wil's dad wasn't actually a jerk and touched that Wil thought he'd like him. "Good." He said with a slight laugh, tone lightening. "It would be a shame if my friend's parent didn't like me."

Wil smiled too. "My moms would adore you." Taylor continued with a fond smile. "Nerdy and queer, their favorite kind of person."

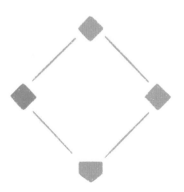

Wil

"I guess I'll have to meet them." Taylor's parents sounded unbelievably cool. And Wil still didn't know any other openly trans people in person. He was almost unreasonably excited to meet them during the family weekend. And not just because they were bringing up costumes for the show.

"You will soon," Taylor said. "Is your dad coming up this weekend as well?"

Wil wondered why he asked. He didn't think there was as much reason for Taylor to be excited about meeting his parent. But maybe he was just curious. "Yeah. He said he would."

Wil was extra nervous for the game because of it. Even after he'd told him, he still didn't want his dad to see just how bad he was. And Taylor had talked Alyx into making him a catcher, so he'd really have the opportunity to mess things up this time.

He tried not to think too much about it. "How does family weekend usually go?" he inquired instead. "It kind of depends on your parents. Some just come for the game, some stay for a meal or whatnot. And, obviously, some kids' families can't come at all. Like Jessie and Mateo. Their folks are all the way out in Grand Junction. Way too far to drive just for the afternoon."

Wil nodded. That made sense.

"Most people who come stay for the game and either lunch or dinner though. That's usually what my moms do." Wil made note of that. He'd have to encourage his dad to do the same and not try to hang around for the whole weekend or anything weird like that. Wil didn't want a repeat of what happened at drop-off. His dad could be a lot if Will didn't warn him off.

He loved his dad, but he hated to admit how nervous he was to see him this weekend. As excited as he was to meet Taylor's moms, he was beginning to realize that he was every bit as worried about seeing his dad. Seeing him in this setting. It was so much of what his dad loved. And Wil still wasn't any good at any of it. How could he not be disappointed?

Taylor

Taylor hefted the overflowing box of costume supplies easily, flanked by his Nanay sporting a couple of her own boxes. His moms really had gone all out, calling on all of their friends and family to loan items. He figured the number of costumes they'd brought could outfit the whole camp three times over.

His Ma held the door to the dorm building open for both of them, kissing his Nanay's cheek as they passed. "You just like that I carry heavy things for you," they observed with a smirk.

"Mhmm. It's the only reason I keep you around." His Ma tossed back casually, "You too, pumpkin." She followed, ruffling Taylor's hair.

Taylor pulled away a bit, but couldn't quite say anything. "Love you too, Ma," he replied instead, finally setting the box down in the lounge area, where it joined four others they'd already brought in.

"Think you brought us enough costumes?" he asked, feeling amused as he surveyed the haul.

"Didn't we tell you, kiddo? There's a whole other carload still in the parking lot." Nanay spoke with a totally straight face. It took the combination of their long pause and Ma's entertained smile to figure out that they were joking.

"Ha, ha, very funny, Nanay." He spoke dryly.

"I missed you, kiddo." His Nanay pulled him into a tight hug, Ma joining in.

"Missed you too. This summer has been awesome." He started talking excitedly, hands flying. "We won our first game. And the variety show is going to be fantastic. We already have a decent number of folks signed up. And my roommate is the best."

His moms listened attentively as he shared everything, words flying fast in his glee to finally get to tell them about everything. "You're going to love Wil," he finished, finally taking a breath, hands dropping when he thought about just how much they would. It really probably would have been easier for them to have a kid like Wil.

"We're excited to meet him," his Nanay agreed with a broad smile, completely unaware of Taylor's own worries. So he aimed to push them aside himself, grabbing both his parents' hands and pulling them toward the stairs.

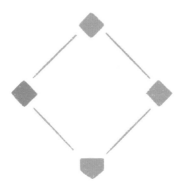

Wil

Wil stayed behind when Taylor went out of the room, smiling wide and texting his parents back as he walked. Wil felt unsure of himself now, for all that he'd been flanking Taylor since he got here. Which, really? That in and of itself wasn't a great realization. Wil had been following him everywhere. And sure Taylor had been humoring him, but would he really have chosen that?

So he stayed behind, feeling worried and uneasy. He'd asked his dad to just come in time for the game, worried about it all being too much. His dad being overbearing or disappointed or... Honestly, Wil had too many fears to count, so it had seemed easiest just to push it back.

He paced fitfully, smiling wryly to himself when he realized he was acting like Taylor. It took longer for Taylor and his parents to get back to the room than Wil had expected but made sense when they did finally show up with a truly ridiculous number of boxes. Taylor was sporting a rainbow boa draped loosely about his neck and a jauntily perched plastic tiara.

You wouldn't think it would be a good look on, well, anyone, but Taylor pulled it off. Or maybe Wil was just hopelessly attracted to him. He looked adorable like that. "Tiara and a t-shirt, interesting combo," Wil observed, feeling awkward.

Taylor did a little spin, posing at the end of it and Wil found himself laughing despite himself. "Cut the theatrics and introduce us to your friend, kiddo." One of his parents nudged him, sounding fond.

"Oh, yeah. Sorry." Taylor said, shifting quickly into what Wil was beginning to recognize as learned mannerisms, almost a performance. It was odd to watch, though Taylor seemed to do it without thinking.

"Wil, this is my Nanay, Jaime. They/them pronouns. And my Ma, Lauren. She/her." He gestured to each of them in turn. His Nanay, Mx. Jaime? Wil wasn't really certain what to call them, was the one who'd prodded Taylor into introductions. A heavyset butch who honestly looked just like Taylor might have if he'd been older with a bit more of a chest.

Taylor's Ma was startlingly tall. He knew that she was tall, but Taylor and his Nanay were already tall enough, and Taylor's Ma still had a good few inches on both of them. She towered over Wil. But she looked nice enough. And she was wearing a Niners shirt which was honestly hilarious.

"Moms, this is Wil." Taylor finished his introduction while Wil was still caught up taking them both in.

"Hi," he managed, with a little wave. "I like your shirt, ma'am."

Taylor's Ma smiled at that. "You didn't tell me he was a Star Trek fan." She teased Taylor with a smile.

"I told you he was a nerd," Taylor protested.

"Hey, we come in many kinds." Jaime held up their hands defensively and then all three of them laughed. They were obviously close. Wil couldn't help but smile at the happy family, even if he felt a bit out of place surrounded by them.

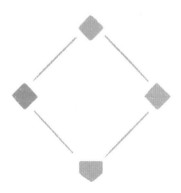

Taylor

Ma thought she was hilarious wearing that t-shirt to at least half his games, for all that ninety-nine percent of the folks there never got the joke. He'd been asked more than once if the Niners played in the Pioneer League or something like that. Clarifying that they were a fictional baseball team in one episode of *Star Trek: Deep Space Nine* never seemed to actually explain much. Most people just left confused.

But, of course, Wil got the reference immediately. He was every bit as big a Trekker as Taylor's moms were. There was something nice about having a friend at camp who could keep up with his moms, rather than just finding them weird.

"When's your dad getting here?" Taylor asked curiously, the game would be starting in less than an hour.

"Oh, right before the match," Wil answered, seeming slightly off. "I think he had to work or something this morning," he continued. Taylor wasn't great at reading folks, but something about the way Wil spoke sounded evasive.

Still, Taylor didn't push, wrapping an arm casually about Wil instead. "Well then, we ought to get down to the field. You got your mitt?" he checked in, waiting for Wil to grab it. He'd already collected his own glove. And the rest of Wil's equipment was loaner stuff that they'd have to get at the locker room.

Taylor led the way down to the field, arm still around Wil. He didn't know what exactly was going on with the guy but wanted to support him however he could. His moms flanked them, chatting happily about everything that had happened since he'd left for camp. Keeping up a steady flow of conversation, they updated him on the latest in their D&D campaign and the news in their friend group. Apparently, Steven was pregnant again, so that was exciting.

Taylor kept an eye on Wil as they walked. He seemed nervous, but then again Taylor was hardly one to talk. He'd distracted himself decently from his normal bout of pre-game nerves by focusing on his moms' arrival, but now that they were this close, he couldn't help but fret. Rubbing his die compulsively, he veered off to the locker room with Wil still in tow.

"We'll come out and see if we can catch Wil's dad before the game starts," he promised, waving goodbye to his moms as they headed towards the stands. Getting ready was the same familiar process it always was. Taylor ran through a basic warm-up routine methodically, before starting to help Wil with some of his gear.

"Wanna see if your dad is here now?" he proposed once they were mostly ready. It was about fifteen minutes until game time, so if he was going to get here for the first pitch he'd pretty much need to be there by then. Wil agreed with a nod and Taylor pulled him out into the stands.

Wil

Wil felt more self-conscious about Taylor's hand in his than he had in the past week or so. The stands packed with adults he didn't know, or rather sporadically filled, made him feel more anxious. Still, he clung to Taylor tightly, more nervous about letting go than he was about holding on.

Wil spotted his dad before he seemed to see them. Sure enough, when his dad actually did catch sight of him it was apparent by the visible double-take he did. Though what exactly he was startled by Wil couldn't have said. His catcher get-up? Him holding Taylor's hand? Taylor holding his hand? There was more than one way that Wil was out of his norm.

Still, his dad recovered correctly. "Wil, you'll never guess who I found," his voice rang out across the stands as he made his way towards them.

 "Councilwoman Weber. Remember I sent you an article about her?" he said with a broad smile gesturing at, surprisingly enough, Taylor's Ma.

"Hello, boys," she greeted them with a smile. "You really can just call me Lauren," she said in an aside to Wil's dad. Wil got the impression it wasn't the first time she'd made that particular correction.

"Nonsense, Councilwoman. What brings you here?" he asked with a smile.

Wil glanced over toward Taylor with an amused look. How exactly his dad had found Taylor's parents of all people he didn't know, but it was certainly funny. "Your Mom is a councilwoman?" he whispered.

"My Ma, yeah. Denver City Council." Taylor returned.

"Your Mom?" Wil's dad remarked with obvious surprise, overhearing the conversation.

"My Ma." Taylor corrected. "Hello. I'm Taylor, he/him pronouns. And, it seems like you've already met my moms." He introduced himself with the same well-practiced style he'd used to conduct introductions earlier.

"Well, isn't that a lovely coincidence?" His dad's smile seemed perpetually plastered to his face. Wil tried to muster the same enthusiasm. Or at least a semblance of it.

"How do you know Taylor's moms?" he asked, still confused.

"I told you. There was an article on the councilwoman. She's the first trans person to ever serve on Denver's city council." He sounded delighted.

That at least explained how he was familiar with her. After Wil came out, his dad had seemed to be on a mission to learn about every vaguely famous trans person in the state. It was sweet, but honestly Wil had started to lose track of all of them after a while.

"First openly trans councilperson," Taylor's Ma corrected, seeming to confuse his dad a bit. But he took it in stride.

"Well, you really are such a role model, ma'am. I'm glad that my boy here is growing up with folks like you he can look up to." He clapped Wil on the back as he spoke, a fond gesture he'd taken up since Wil came out. Wil didn't necessarily mind it, but it did always feel a bit odd.

"Well, it's a pleasure to meet Wil's father," Taylor's Nanay said, carrying off the conversation. "We already had the opportunity to talk to him a bit ago when we arrived. Taylor and Wil are roommates this summer, you know?"

Taylor

Well, Taylor hadn't expected that, but it was actually kind of cute. It was always nice to find folks who were fans of his Ma. Goodness knew, he was proud of her, for all that most people just didn't bother with following local politics.

Wil's dad seemed nice. And he clearly adored Wil. Taylor liked him, for what first impressions were worth. Still, it was even harder than usual to make small talk with the game looming. Instead, he found himself listening quietly to their parents' exchange, his die in one hand and Wil's hand still in the other.

Unsurprisingly, Nanay was already recommending some local resources for parents of trans kids. They always had a running list of them that they could rattle off the top of their head. Meanwhile, Wil's dad, Scott, was offering to help them follow the game. Taylor didn't know that it would make much difference, but it was still a kind offer.

At some point, he'd have to try his D&D explanation on them. If any method of explaining the sport would actually make sense to his moms it would have to be that one. He'd certainly tried defining baseball terminology and walking them through the rules more than once before.

Finally, Alyx blew a whistle calling them in for a huddle and they had an excuse to pull away, joining all the other kids racing out of the stands and down toward the field. They were far from the only ones visiting with parents or other family members until the last possible moment.

Taylor did enjoy visiting with family. He just knew that at this point his nerves would get worse and worse until the game was actually done. And basic social niceties were challenging enough when he wasn't hyperfocused on an upcoming game.

He and Wil were both starting players. Alyx always put a

solid mix of more experienced players and newbies into the starting lineup. After all, the whole point of the camp was to give everyone lots of playtime. Wil still seemed nervous, but there was little more Taylor could do at this point. He wrapped him in a quick hug, amused at the realization that Wil was so much smaller than he was. He could still get his arms all the way around him, protective vest and all.

"Good game," Taylor wished him before jogging out to the pitcher's mound. The first couple innings went by quickly. Taylor's throw felt off and he found himself growing more annoyed as the game went on. He was allowing hits that he should be able to avoid. By the middle of the third inning, he'd walked two players and allowed three runs and was solidly frustrated.

"People walk. It's not the end of the world, Taylor." Alyx tried to reassure him when he was on the bench, but he shrugged her words off. "Everyone has off days, and even the best pitchers walk batters." He knew that she was trying to be supportive, but at the moment it was just more to process.

Wil

Wil hated seeing how upset Taylor looked. He wished there was something he could do to support him, but he seemed completely caught up in his own thoughts. Scowling down at his hands, die flying quickly between them.

He was still kind of amazed that he understood what a "walk" was now. When a batter gets four pitches that they couldn't reasonably hit—called "balls," confusingly—then they just get to go to first base. Wil didn't envy Taylor his position in the slightest. It seemed impossible. You have to throw a ball so that someone can conceivably hit it, but also make it difficult to hit. Wil still counted himself lucky if he managed to throw a ball in the general direction he'd intended.

Taylor seemed amazing to him, even on an "off day," but clearly he didn't feel the same way himself. Wil was just starting to make his way closer, wanting to offer Taylor something. Some kind of support or a friendly word, even if he didn't know what on earth he would actually say. But he was interrupted by Alyx.

"You're up, Wil," she said with a wide smile, tossing a bat his way as soon as he'd turned around. Wil did a double-take. It was only the third inning. He had completely lost track of the lineup, but he didn't expect to have to bat yet. Last game he didn't have to bat until nearly the end when Alyx pulled out a starting player and put him in.

"Go get 'em, tiger." She waved him off cheerily, seemingly completely unconcerned that he was useless at baseball. Sure, Wil had gotten better at batting, but that was one-on-one with Taylor or, worst-case scenario, at a team practice. Not in front of all these people. Not in front of his dad. Not with Taylor already in a foul mood.

Wil knew his anxiety was hurting him, but he couldn't help it. He just didn't trust himself. The first pitch he swung too early. "Strike one!" Breathing deeply, he tried to recover, but he overcorrected, swinging way too late. "Strike two!" Why did they have the umpire yelling so close to him? How was anyone supposed to concentrate during that? He tried so hard to block out everything, forcing himself to breathe slowly.

On the third pitch, he watched the timing as close as he could, swinging out at just the right moment. And making contact with absolutely nothing. The pitch went wide, there was nothing to hit. He shouldn't have swung for it. "Strike three! You're out," the umpire called. Wil clutched the bat tightly as he walked back to the dugout, cheeks flushed.

He put in so much effort. And he had gotten better. But it didn't mean a thing if he couldn't control his anxiety. He'd done terribly. And the worst thing of all was that he knew he could have done better. At least, he could have if he wasn't such a mess.

"Good try," Alyx said, smile completely undisturbed as she took his bat back from them. "Take a break, dude. You'll get another go at them." And goodness, he'd almost forgotten about that. He would have to do that again. And no doubt he'd be just as awful. His teammates must hate him.

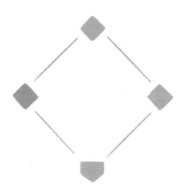

Taylor

By the fourth inning, Jessie's team was up by three runs and Taylor was feeling worse and worse. But, he rubbed his die as he walked out, single-mindedly focused. Running his fingers over the indented numbers. He found the side numbered "20" by feel. He focused on it. The first batter up was a kid he'd been playing against since Little League. Taylor stretched. He could do this.

He struck Tyrell out. And that felt good. He hadn't actually pulled off a strikeout yet this game, but he could feel himself getting into the swing of it now. The next batter managed to hit the ball, but it was a pop fly and easily caught.

After that Taylor managed two more strikes. The batter finally made contact on the third pitch. It was a decent hit but easily returned. He got tagged out on first. Taylor rolled his shoulders as he walked off. That felt like better baseball. He was finally starting to get on a roll.

But the moment he got off the field, Alyx pulled him aside. "Nice job, Taylor. You take a break now. I'm putting Jesed in for the fifth." Taylor deflated. He knew that it wasn't strictly about his pitching. They always liked to give as many kids as possible chances to play at camp. And Jesed was a good pitcher. She absolutely deserved the playtime.

But he'd gotten four innings and he'd all but wasted them. He was going off with his team behind and nothing much to show for his pitching. And that feeling sucked. He trudged slowly to the bench, sinking on to it slowly. Nothing much left for him to do this game then.

That could be the hardest part of being taken out. Now all he could do was just sit there and watch. Sometimes Taylor enjoyed it. He liked watching baseball. But right now he could only stew in his own disappointment.

Still, he tried to pull himself up and focus on the game. They still had time to pull ahead. And he wanted to see Wil's catching when he wasn't out on the field himself. By the start of the sixth, he'd made his way over to stand by Alyx, watching his teammates take their positions on the field.

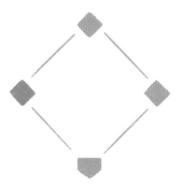

Wil

Wil still felt a bit odd as a catcher. It was so different than being in the outfield, though the part of him that always hated PE was glad not to have to jog way out there every inning. So far, it felt like he was just existing. He didn't think he'd messed anything up yet, but he also couldn't see how he was helping.

He just caught the ball when the batter didn't manage to hit it and threw it back. It was a pretty simple rhythm to get into. He was also supposed to get the ball and tag people out before they could make it to home plate, but he hadn't actually managed to do that yet, much less manage any of the strategy pieces Taylor claimed made him perfect for this position.

The ball and the bat and all the things flying around his head were still pretty scary, but he did appreciate all of the safety equipment. It made him less likely to want to duck and run the moment he saw a ball headed his way. That was exactly what he had done through years of PE classes growing up and the exact opposite of what you're apparently supposed to do in literally any sport other than dodgeball.

Their team was losing and Wil knew he should be disappointed about that. Everyone else seemed to be. But, honestly, he mostly just wanted to avoid messing up too badly himself. By the sixth inning, he was starting to feel pretty confident that he was actually a decent catcher. Nothing stellar, but he hadn't failed dramatically in the way he'd been certain he would. Only two more innings and it would be over.

He was still thinking about that. Waiting for the pitcher to throw the ball. They always seemed to take forever stretching or blowing bubble gum or adjusting their hat or whatever else was apparently crucial to do before pitching. Taylor had told him once that baseball players were, as a rule, all incredibly superstitious. Wil was definitely learning that was true.

By the time he noticed the runner stealing, she was already halfway to third. He tried to signal Jesed, but it was way too late. She'd barely gotten turned around by the time the runner slid onto third base. This was the whole reason Taylor had recommended him for the position. And, sure enough, he'd failed. Every bit as spectacularly as he'd imagined.

The first player stealing all game, and he missed it. He'd honestly forgotten that he was even supposed to be watching for that. Off in his own little world just waiting for the next pitch. Thinking that he actually made a decent catcher of all things. Wasn't that ironic?

He barely made it through the rest of the inning. All he could think about was his dad watching. His dad had been a catcher. He'd probably caught countless runners stealing. And his first time ever watching his son play baseball, Wil had failed.

Taylor

Two runs down going into the bottom of the seventh. Taylor fidgeted with his die incessantly. He had no idea why Alyx wasn't more on edge. She still had the same relaxed posture and easy smile she always did. Wil was first at bat. Taylor helped him get his vest off and sent him up to bat with a thumbs up.

Wil was never going to be a phenomenal batter, but he really had gotten reasonably good at it. He was good at reading where a pitch would go, which was an invaluable skill. He just had to trust himself. Taylor watched proudly as he got into position. The difference between the awkward boy he'd met a couple of weeks ago who didn't even know how to hold a bat and now was plain as day.

The first pitch was far outside of the strike zone. Wil took it in stride, bat barely moving. "Ball!" The umpire called out, and Taylor nodded proudly. Wil had read that perfectly. There was no way he could have hit that ball.

The next pitch Wil missed, but barely. He was a teeny bit too high, but he'd swung at the perfect time. And Taylor was still so proud of him. He knew that Wil didn't really care about this sport, but he'd worked so hard at it.

The third was a fastball as good as any Taylor could throw on his best days. And, as proud as he was of Wil, he was already expecting a strike. A pitch that fast challenged far more talented batters.

Wil made contact with a resounding crack. And sure the ball went wide and was almost immediately called foul, but still, Wil had hit that ball. Taylor knew he couldn't have; he was a terrible batter.

Wil struck out swinging moments after and made his way off the field. "Way to go." Taylor pulled Wil into a hug as soon as he reached the dugout.

"What do you mean? I struck out." Wil said, sounding confused. Now that he was closer, Taylor could see his cheeks were flushed and his eyes looked damp.

"Yeah. But, that fastball. I couldn't believe you made contact with it!" Taylor continued excitedly.

"It was a foul ball. Might as well not have swung at all for all it was worth," Wil protested.

"Well, sure, it didn't get you on base. Don't tell me you could have come close to hitting that pitch two weeks ago though," he argued, still grinning. "And there's still two outs left. We could always pull ahead. It's not over 'til it's over."

Wil

Wil shrugged off Taylor's praise. He'd struck out. Didn't even manage a decent hit. Everything Taylor was saying felt completely disingenuous. Trying to talk up the pathetic nerdy kid who was useless at baseball. Well-meaning as it may have been, it just made him feel worse.

He was still distracted, feeling sorry for himself when Taylor started whooping and cheering next to him. "What happened?" Wil asked, feeling confused. "Shonda doubled!" Taylor explained almost bouncing with excitement. "See? I told you we were still in it." Sure enough, Wil could see Shonda panting on second base. He didn't understand how anyone ran that fast, no matter how far you hit the ball.

For all that Wil imagined the poor girl must be completely out of breath, Shonda still managed to steal third a couple of pitches later. And honestly, the fact that the other team's catcher didn't seem to realize it until too late made Wil feel a bit better, though not much.

The next batter struck out and Wil turned towards Taylor, wanting to comfort him. Shonda had been doing awesome, but at this point, that didn't seem worth much. It was hard to believe that anything could really change this late in the game. They were still nearly done. Yet oddly enough Taylor seemed relatively fine. On edge, but not too disappointed. "Time for some two-out baseball," he proclaimed, D20 weaving through his fingers.

Sure enough, Chase managed a hit and made it to first. Shonda ran home, and all of a sudden they were only one run behind. Jordan was next at bat, and it almost seemed like he'd make it. He hit the ball and he was almost to first base when an outfielder caught it and that was it.

Wil looked to Taylor for confirmation, trying to ensure that he was following a game he still didn't completely understand. "We lost, yeah?" he asked, finding Taylor's expression inscrutable.

"Yeah." Taylor sighed. "Darn. That was a close one." He headed back towards the bench and Wil found himself trailing.

Taylor

Taylor was a sore loser. He knew that and it was not something he liked about himself. It didn't make it any less true. He hated losing. And he knew full well Jessie would be teasing from the moment they shook hands on the field.

He loved her to pieces. They'd been friends for years and he knew that teasing was how she showed affection. Everyone did. Just look at her and Mateo's friendship. It didn't change the fact that her teasing plus his usual post-loss sulking wasn't the best mix.

He was dour and quiet after the game, squeezing his die tightly, the edges of it digging sharply into his palm. Still, he let himself drift toward the stands with the crowd, accepting his moms' hugs and high-fives. They were both used to his usual post-loss blues and didn't try to get too much of a reaction from him.

Wil's dad was still with them. Taylor got the impression they'd been talking all game. He was glad their parents seemed to get along. "Wow. You're quite some pitcher, kid." He complimented Taylor with a broad smile.

Taylor forced his own polite well-rehearsed smile, feeling awkward and uncomfortable talking to someone he barely knew. Especially someone complimenting him after he'd pitched a pretty lousy game. "Thanks," he managed.

"Dinner?" Taylor suggested, feeling antsy and trapped. He wanted to get out of the stands. Crowds were difficult for him at the best of times. The group agreed readily, starting to weave through people and move in the general direction of the dining hall.

Taylor let himself trail behind once they were out of the stands, still feeling overwhelmed. He was coming down from his game-time excitement and processing his disappointment all at once. He felt the tears on his face before he even realized that he needed to cry. He knew he'd be fine. He was overwhelmed more than anything else. His emotions often caught him off guard.

Taylor noticed Nanay looking back at him but waved them ahead. He just needed a moment. They trusted him and continued on, arm linked through Ma's still talking animatedly with Wil's dad. Wil himself still hung behind though. Taylor tried to wave him forward too, but Wil ignored him, making his way closer to Taylor.

Taylor pulled his shoulders up. He just needed a break. Seriously. Was that too much to ask for? He felt like if he had to talk to one more person at that moment he'd break down and never make it through dinner in the awful dining hall. "Please, just go," he managed to get out, putting all his energy into figuring out the words.

Wil

Wil saw Taylor crying and he was struck with so much concern. He knew how much Taylor cared. And how much it hurt him when they lost games in practice. Now, he'd lost again, in front of his parents. That must be even worse.

Wil wanted to comfort him, wanted to pull him into a hug, and tell him how loved he is. But he moved closer and Taylor physically pulled away. And he tried not to take it too seriously, to hover at a slight distance. But then Taylor outright told him to leave, sounding angry and shuttered.

And it hit Wil all at once. It was his fault. If he'd just caught that runner. If he'd just prevented her from stealing, they wouldn't have made that run. The game would have been tied and gone into extra innings. Taylor had been so excited to find something Wil could do. That he thought Wil could do. He'd put so much time into helping and teaching Wil. And then Wil had failed. Of course he was angry with him. Why wouldn't he be?

Wil went into the dining hall slowly, forcing his feelings down deep. Trying to prepare himself to make small talk with Taylor's parents. Trying to prepare himself for his dad's reaction. Wow. His dad. He must have disappointed him too. Even if he never said anything. Wil had so dearly wanted to just not mess up. And he couldn't even manage that.

Their parents waved him over immediately, still seeming bright and cheery. But Wil knew how his dad must really feel. He honestly ignored him somewhat, focusing on Taylor's parents. He'd been so eager to meet them. He tried to actually enjoy it.

It was hard though. He'd thought that he and Taylor were becoming friends. That they'd be able to hang out after camp. Wil liked him. He wanted to be a part of his life. But, that didn't really feel possible now. So, what was the point of getting to know his parents anyways?

When Taylor did come in, he seemed perfectly neutral. But Wil could tell that he wasn't himself. His mannerisms were too perfect, too practiced. Nothing like the guy Wil had gotten to know as Taylor had gradually relaxed around him.

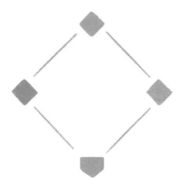

Taylor

Jessie and Mateo caught up with Taylor by the time he had grounded himself, each looping a friendly arm around him. He let himself be swept forward by them, feeling less overwhelmed and on the brink of a meltdown now. Jessie's smirk and teasing comments were still hard, but he'd certainly had enough practice giving the right cavalier response.

The three of them got their food and joined the group already seated. Jessie and Mateo greeted Taylor's moms casually as ever and introduced themselves to Wil's dad. They only really ever saw one another at camp and over video calls, but it didn't stop the two of them from knowing just about everything there was to know about Taylor's family, and they joined the conversation easily.

Taylor mostly ate his food quietly. He was well-practiced at giving the appropriate responses at the right time in conversations he wasn't engaged in, and he was able to focus most of his energy on his plate. Forcing himself to eat enough food could be tough when he felt overwhelmed. It all got so bad sensory-wise any time he was in this headspace.

Wil was getting along well with his moms, cracking jokes about theater and D&D. They clearly adored him every bit as much as Taylor had expected. Meanwhile, Wil's dad, while chiming into the conversation occasionally, stayed quieter. He looked so proud, Taylor thought. He was clearly so happy to be here, spending time with his son.

After dinner, the kids walked with their parents out to their cars. As they approached Taylor's moms' car, Wil's face lit up with a smile. "This is you?" he said.

"Yeah," replied Taylor's Ma. "She's old but reliable. We've had many, many road trips in this car."

"The queer bumper stickers," said Wil. "I saw them on the first day. They made me feel a little less nervous. Like maybe I wouldn't be as alone as I thought. And then I wasn't." He smiled at Taylor. There seemed like something was off about his smile, but Taylor couldn't put his finger on it.

"Well, you're welcome to visit anytime," she said. "May I hug you?" Wil nodded and was embraced in one of her tight hugs. Taylor's Nanay held out their hand for a fist bump, which Wil returned with a smile.

Then, Taylor's moms turned to him. "We love you so much, sweetie. Hug?" Taylor let himself be pulled into one of their signature group hugs.

When they finally let go, his Ma reached out to ruffle his hair again, but Taylor ducked and muttered, "Don't please," under his breath.

His moms glanced at each other, but his Ma pulled her hand back and smiled at him. "Fist bump?"

"Sure," he said, laughing when she ducked her hand out of the way at the last second, leaving him pushing his fist into empty air.

"Gotcha!" she said triumphantly, while Nanay cracked up next to her. "We'll see you in a week, kiddo. Throw... fast? I guess?"

Taylor laughed. "Thanks. See you soon." He stepped back as they backed out of the parking spot and waved as they pulled away.

Wil

After escaping Taylor's Ma's wonderful but very tight hug, Wil turned to his dad to say goodbye. "Thanks for coming," he said.

"Of course," his dad replied. "I always love a good baseball game, and it was great to see you out there. You've learned so much."

Wil knew that was code for "you're not completely awful," but he smiled and said, "Thanks."

His dad clapped him on the shoulder and smiled, before getting into his car. The window rolled down, he called out, "See you next week, son. Keep your eye on the ball."

Wil waved, and once his dad was out of sight, turned back to Taylor, who had his eyes on the pavement. "Back to the room?" he said, and Taylor nodded, still not looking at him. Wil sighed, resigned knowing he'd ruined his chance with his only friend here.

They walked back in silence. Wil kept trying to think of a way to start a conversation. He and Taylor still had to live together for the next week. No matter how much he'd disappointed Taylor, he still wanted things to be less weird and awkward between them.

Taylor stayed utterly silent though, mouth set and eyes forward. He didn't even look at Wil. When they did finally make it back to their dorm room, he collapsed wordlessly on the bed, reaching for his headphones.

"Do you need anything?" Wil found himself offering awkwardly, concern welling up and overriding his own feelings of hurt and disappointment for a moment. Taylor was so obviously having such a rough time. He'd pretty much shut down the moment their parents had pulled away.

"No." Taylor looked almost surprised. As if he'd forgotten that Wil was even there.

 And honestly, why not? It's not like Wil was worth much. Still, he wanted to try. "Just, if I can help with anything. I want to be able to support you," he rambled awkwardly.

Taylor's expression didn't change. "I really just need space." He spoke brusquely, pushing Wil away just the same as he had earlier. Wil's heart broke a bit with that. He didn't even bother with trying to stop the tears that welled up from falling.

"Okay. Fine. Just hate me, then," he snapped, feeling hurt and angry. He was mad at himself for messing up so much, but also mad at Taylor. He'd trusted him. But apparently, he shouldn't have.

Taylor

"Hate you?" Taylor reacted with surprise, barely noticing Wil's tears. "What the heck?" He really didn't have the energy for this right now. Today had been absolutely exhausting. "All I want is a break. Aren't I allowed to have half an hour of quiet?" he shouted back, knowing he was too loud. It felt impossible to regulate volume right then.

"Sorry you got saddled with me," Wil yelled back, beginning to full-on cry.

Taylor just felt so lost. He hated when people apologized without a clear reason. It was so confusing and impossible to navigate. "What are you even apologizing for?" He didn't know how he was supposed to respond.

"I never should have ended up at this stupid camp, and I'm sorry that I ended up here with you." Wil's face was red and he was still so loud. Taylor had no idea what he'd done so wrong, but it was clear that Wil was furious with him.

"I can leave," he offered. Still desperate to just get somewhere quiet and have a chance to think. And, so confused about what he'd done wrong and where all this was coming from. "I can just leave," Taylor repeated, no idea what else to say.

"I'm sure you never wanted to be around me anyway." Wil snapped, turning away from him. "Fine. Go wherever you want. I don't care," he continued in a quieter voice, the words sounding short and clipped. Taylor just nodded, gathering his earbuds and phone with one hand and his backpack with another.

He could go camp out with Mateo and Jessie if he really needed to, but for now, he just wanted to get away. He escaped to a small lounge at the end of the hall and turned all of the lights off, collapsing down onto a couch and trying to figure out what on earth had gone wrong.

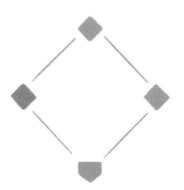

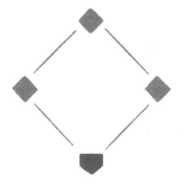

Part Four

Wil

Wil fell asleep before Taylor came back that night, tears staining his pillow. Things had been going so well with them, and of course, Wil had to ruin it. If only he was better at baseball, he wouldn't be such a letdown. He woke up early and watched TikToks in an attempt to distract himself, mostly unsuccessfully.

Taylor got dressed silently and left for breakfast without him. After a while, Wil followed, but Taylor had left the dining hall already. Maybe that was for the best, Wil thought, eating his cereal alone in the corner before heading to morning practice.

"Good morning, Sluggers!" Alyx exclaimed cheerfully. "Look, I know some of you are probably disappointed," looking at the team. Glancing around, Wil saw that they all looked as dejected as he felt. Taylor was off by himself, still not looking anywhere near him. "But," Alyx continued, "You have to remember that it's not just about winning; it's about having fun! And I've seen so much improvement from all of you, I am so proud. Now let's get to practice!"

They started with their usual warm-up stretches and then paired up to practice throwing and catching. Wil was paired with Jesed, the pitcher that had taken over for Taylor in the last game. She was pretty, with dark hair in two shoulder-length braids. They threw the ball back and forth for a while, then moved on to batting and fielding, and played a few practice innings against Jessie's team in the afternoon. Wil resolutely avoided Taylor all day, determined to stay out of his way.

They had some free time before dinner, and Wil, unsure what else to do, called his dad. It was nice feeling like he could just call him for help. Tearily, he found himself explaining the whole messed up situation, voice hitching and face wet. But somehow he didn't feel as embarrassed as he would have once.

He knew his dad wouldn't think any less of him for crying. "And I just don't know how to fix it." He finished finally. "I really like him, Dad. Sure, we're not gonna date or anything, but we were becoming friends. Now I messed it all up."

"Wait for just a second, Wil." His dad's voice was warm and calming and Wil forced himself to take a breath. "Why are you blaming all this on yourself?" he asked. Wil blinked. Of course, it was his fault. He'd just explained. He'd lost the game and he was so useless at baseball and pretty useless in general and why would Taylor want to spend time with someone like him anyway?

Dad must have known how his thoughts were spiraling because he spoke again. "Listen, it's not your fault that your team lost the game. Teams lose. You still played your best, didn't you?" Wil nodded to himself. He really had.

"I tried so hard."

"I don't know this boy of yours that well, but I do know that if he's the type to cut you off just because you're not as good a baseball player as he is, he's not worth having in your life." His dad spoke resolutely. "But Wil, kiddo, I don't know Taylor. You know him better than me, and even then it's only been a couple of weeks. But from what you've told me, he sounded like a nice kid. Are you really certain that's how he feels?"

"I guess... I guess not," Wil responded. Maybe he had been jumping to conclusions. He'd just been so sure that it was all his fault.

"Don't make assumptions, son. Talk to him. There may be something else going on. And make certain he knows your feelings as well." Wil nodded, more confidently this time.

"Thanks, Dad." It was good advice, and in his dad's solid straightforward way of speaking it made sense. Wil could do that. Probably.

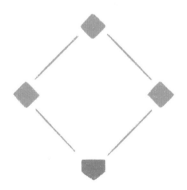

Taylor

Taylor hated this. He hated how easily he seemed to mess relationships up. He wasn't great at friendship. He was fine at day-to-day social interaction. He could mask perfectly well for short periods of time. Taylor had lots of acquaintances, teammates, and people in his classes, folks he liked just fine and dandy.

But more meaningful social relationships had always been tough for him. He did better with adults or little kids. People far enough off in age from him that it was okay to be a bit disconnected. And he had Mateo and Jessie. They lived far enough away that most of their interaction was via text which was easier for him.

His friendships always seemed to go sour one way or another. He was just a little bit too weird. His brain didn't work the same way other kids' did and that led to issues. He knew logically that it wasn't his fault. Or theirs for that matter. It just sucked sometimes.

He was easy and happy around Wil because he was a little bit different too. Anxious and nerdy and queer. Wil was closer to the kind of people he could relate to. Taylor had always done best with other disabled people, but sometimes it was tough to find disabled kids. At least ones who lived close to him.

He didn't know what he'd done, but it was obvious that Wil was hurting. Taylor hadn't intended that, but it was true nonetheless. And now he didn't have the slightest idea how to fix it. Or if it even could be fixed.

He caught his die, squeezing it tightly letting the edges poke into his palm, and stared up at the empty top bunk. He had grabbed some food and retreated to his room after practice to get some quiet. He got his phone from the side table, cued up some thunderstorm noises, and worked on settling his mind.

He needed to do something, if only so that he and Wil could get through the rest of camp together reasonably. But first he needed to take care of himself. Letting his thoughts spiral through everything challenging for him wasn't going to help.

Eventually, he started to feel more in control. He relaxed his grip on the die, rolling it between his fingers again, still focusing on the gentle rain noises, making himself actively pay attention to the sound of it. He took a breath, then another. Finally, he sat up again.

The first step was trying to get a better understanding of what was actually happening. Taylor threw on a jacket and headed towards the door. Pacing through the dorm room would just get him riled up again. He needed to go for a walk. Wil had been shouting about not being good enough and assuming that Taylor didn't want to be friends with him.

Obviously, that wasn't true. Taylor knew that part of that was likely just Wil's anxiety, but he worried that it was also something he'd done. Something he'd said or not said or some kind of nonverbal thing he didn't even realize that he was doing that Wil interpreted that way.

He spent a long time walking and thinking. It was late evening by the time he finally headed back towards the dorm, aware that everyone would be expected to be in for curfew soon.

At this point, he and Wil just needed to sit down and actually talk through things. But Taylor thought he might have an idea of what was going on. And, if so, he had a thought that he hoped would help.

Wil

"Thanks, babe," Wil said fondly. Leila always was chill with him just needing to cry and be upset for a while. He appreciated it so much. Talking to his dad was helpful. He'd already felt calmer after having a chance to explain everything to him.

But he also knew that he needed to spend some more time just being upset before he could have any kind of helpful conversation with Taylor, so he called Leila. She was a darling as usual. And after Wil got all of his hard feelings out, they spent some time just catching up.

He felt way better by the time she had to go. Hanging up, he looked around the lounge. He'd been in here for literally hours by now. He really ought to go back to the room and at least check in with Taylor. He stood slowly and gathered all his things, which had gradually ended up strewn about him and straightened the couch cushions before heading out.

He was kind of surprised to find the room empty when he did get there, tentatively opening the door following a quiet knock. He knew it was his space too; still, it felt weird now. Taylor's absence didn't help. He just wanted to work through things, but by himself there wasn't much that he could do.
Still, it was nearly curfew, so he'd have to be back soon. Wouldn't he? Wil tried not to fret too much, climbing up to sit on his bunk and swinging his legs nervously. He tried to force himself to read but didn't have much luck focusing. He gave up and put on music instead.

Eventually, the door swung open and Taylor came in, obviously fidgeting with the die in his pocket. Wil was relieved to see him. "Hey," Wil said hesitantly. Taylor looked up at him and returned the greeting. "Listen can we..." Wil stopped when he realized that Taylor was speaking at the same time.

"Are you up for talking?" Taylor asked.

Wil nodded, unable to hold back a chuckle. Great minds think alike. "Talking would be great." He spoke with relief, pausing the music and swinging down from the bed.

"I'm sorry," Wil found himself saying. "I'm sorry. You've been so nice to me and I really like you and just ... I'm sorry."

Taylor looked at him for an extended period of time, eyes calculating but little on his face to give Wil any idea what he might be thinking. "What are you sorry for?" he finally asked, speaking slowly.

Wil blinked. He didn't know. Everything? He tried to remember his dad's advice. Tried not to assume that Taylor actually hated him and all the nonsense his anxiety might like him to believe. "I'm sorry that I yelled at you," he ended up saying. "That wasn't fair."

Taylor nodded. "I'm sorry too." He spoke seriously. "I'm sorry that I snapped and got so upset the other day. I was just really stressed and overwhelmed after the game, but I shouldn't have taken it out on you. And I'm sorry if I put too much pressure on you or anything like that." His words were quiet and even. "I think I did, didn't I?" he asked, looking down at Wil inquiringly. Wil shrugged, it all seemed kind of silly now. Yet he knew just how scared and upset he had been. "I think so. But it wasn't just you." He leaned against the desk. "I just feel so useless here sometimes. I'm better at baseball than I was, but I'm never gonna be good at it."

He could feel tears welling up again and didn't bother trying to stop them. Taylor wordlessly rummaged through his backpack, and then passed him a pack of tissues. Wil took them with a grateful smile.

"You know, you don't have to be good at something to do it?" Taylor said after a long moment of shared silence, smiling slightly himself. "It's okay to just have fun." He chuckled. "Or, well, I know baseball isn't really your idea of fun either. But you can still do it even if you're not very good."

Taylor

He wasn't certain of himself. Taylor always wanted to fix everything. And sometimes that was less than helpful. But he hoped that maybe this would be. Plus it would be fun. At least, he'd have fun with it.

"I had an idea?" he said, intentionally shifting the inflection to turn it into a question. He waited for Wil to nod before he continued. "I know it can be scary to do things that you're not good at. And it's okay if it's hard. But you can, and I don't know if this would help."

He tried to fight the urge to over-explain, aware that Wil still didn't know what he was thinking. "We could do a duet together at the variety show?" he proposed. "I'm a rubbish singer, but I really enjoy it. And, well, maybe it would be nice to feel like you're not the only one doing something you're not great at in front of everyone."

He wished he could read Wil's expression better, but reading people's expressions had never been a talent of his. He just had to wait for Wil to say whatever he thought. For the moment, Wil wasn't saying anything though. So, Taylor continued. "I also would like it. Singing with you. I like doing things with you."

Wil finally nodded. "That would be a lot of fun," he said. Taylor still couldn't entirely make out his tone, but it sounded positive. "I like doing things with you too." At that Taylor finally began to relax, a small smile forming. They still had things they needed to figure out. But it was nice to hear that Wil still liked him. Maybe still wanted to be friends even.

"I... what do you need? Do you know what would be helpful?" he asked. "I don't want to make you feel bad about yourself." He didn't know if he'd done something to contribute to Wil's anxiety. He never was good at social nuance.

Wil took his time, obviously considering the question. "I think less coaching and more just practicing," he said finally, Taylor nodded intently. "I appreciated it at first, when I still wasn't even clear on the rules. But, now, it just ends up feeling like a lot of pressure."

That made sense. He still felt a lot of pressure about games himself, but he knew that was him. He didn't want Wil to feel like that too. It was helpful to know what specifically he needed.

"And, yeah, reassurance sometimes when I'm struggling," Wil said, ducking his eyes down, cheeks flushing. Taylor took a step closer, wanting to offer comfort of some kind but still uncertain how it may be received.

"I'm not good at that." He spoke frankly, feeling a bit self-conscious. "Reassurance I can do. That's great. Thanks for letting me know it would be helpful. But knowing when you're struggling." Taylor clarified. "I can perform most emotions and whatever the way people expect me to, but I'm still not great at reading those cues in other people. Like, tone and body language and all that. It's pretty hard and even if I know something is wrong, I struggle with figuring out what."

Taylor trusted Wil. It was nice realizing that he still did trust him. Still, he kind of felt weird that this stuff was hard for him. Normally he didn't mind it much, but it was difficult when it impacted his relationships. He liked being autistic; it would just be nice if everyone else could be less confusing.

Wil nodded seriously. "That makes sense. I could try to tell you?" he proposed after a moment. "I don't know that I'll always be able to. But when I'm having a hard time, I can try to ask for reassurance. Or at least let you know it would be nice."

"Sounds like a good plan." This is why he'd liked Wil in the first place. He was good with how Taylor's brain operated. He wasn't weird about it.

"I'm thinking now that there may have been things going on before we actually fought the other day," Taylor said directly. "But I didn't notice them beforehand. I didn't have any idea you were upset." He shared.

Wil nodded. "I tend to kind of bottle things up," he said quietly. And, well, Taylor could certainly relate to that.

"Me too," he said wryly. "Though I'm not great at hiding them. People still know when I'm upset."

Wil laughed. "Yeah. I have kind of noticed that," he said.

Taylor laughed as well. "What? My post-loss sulking isn't subtle?" It was difficult sometimes, but he was mostly okay joking about it. He knew he felt emotions really strongly and he tried not to act like a jerk because of it. But, yeah, it was a pretty established fact. He and his moms joked about it together too.

Wil

"I could... I could use some reassurance now." Wil forced himself to say. It was even harder than he imagined it would be when he'd first suggested it. He felt weird and guilty about needing reassurance, and it didn't feel like something he deserved. Still, he wanted to try.

And Taylor still made him feel safe, even after everything. He was watching Wil silently, just waiting. Not asking or pushing. Nothing on his face indicated that he thought Wil was weird or wrong. And that helped. Wil breathed shakily "You still wanna be friends?" he mumbled quietly, struggling to get the words out.

Taylor seemed to take a moment to process, but then he was nodding. "I'd really like that. I like you, Wil. I want to be friends with you."

That was all Wil needed to hear. "I'm glad," he said after taking a moment to simply process that they were actually okay. "I want to be friends with you too," he added. "I'm glad we met."

Taylor spread out his arms. "Hug?" he asked, and Wil didn't even bother with a response, he let himself fall into Taylor gratefully. Taylor's arms wrapped around him snuggly, encompassing him easily and Wil felt so content and safe, letting himself be held.

After a long moment, Taylor released him. "And, uh, Wil?" he said, tapping his fingers rapidly against his palm. "About that crush thing?"

"Yeah?" Wil said, nervously, his face heating up. He had honestly been hoping that Taylor had forgotten and they wouldn't have to talk about it again.

"Just so you know. I really appreciate you telling me about that. And I trust you too, so I wanted to tell you. I think I might be aromantic? I'm not sure, and I don't feel like I need to be right now? But I wanted to share. I'm really glad I get to be your friend." Taylor's hands came to a sudden stop, clasped together and he took some deep breaths.

Wil took Taylor's hand, squeezing it lightly. He was a bit sad, but at least now he could focus on being Taylor's friend. And he felt kind of amazed that Taylor had felt comfortable sharing that with him. Wil smiled. "Thanks for letting me know. I'm happy I get to be your friend too."

"Wanna listen to music?" Wil proposed, holding his phone up. Taylor nodded, and he pressed play. It was easy now. Easy to both start dancing and singing along and just existing together. Dorky and fun and comfortable like they had been. They both stayed up far too late just having fun, trying to mute the music any time they thought they heard a floor leader walking about after curfew.

"So, duet?" Wil asked again the next morning. They were on their way to breakfast, side by side shoulders brushing against one another. Back to normal. It had only been a couple of days, but it had sucked. Wil was grateful that it was easy to be close to Taylor again.

Taylor smiled wide. "If you want to. You've heard me sing." He reminded Wil. He sounded light and comfortable. Still, Wil wondered if he had any fear and anxiety tucked in there as well. It could be hard sometimes to tell what Taylor really felt and what he was just performing.

When he first met Taylor, it seemed like he had everything together. He could talk about gender and emotions and stuff in such fancy words. And he just seemed so comfortable with himself. Now Wil was starting to realize that he was every bit as complex and messy as anyone else. He liked that about him. "I'd love to. I have a blast singing together," he said fondly, thinking about how cute Taylor looked when he got really into a song. He could be so passionate, not holding anything back. It was absolutely adorable. "The big question—" Wil continued, "is what song?"

Taylor

The last few days had been ridiculously busy. Between the variety show and baseball practice and all of the normal hustle and bustle of the last week of camp, Taylor sometimes questioned why he'd thought adding anything else to this was a good idea.

But, tired and overwhelmed as he was, he couldn't bring himself to regret it. He sat on the floor of Jessie and Mateo's dorm room at 2:00 a.m. with them and Wil prepping programs at the last minute, well aware that the counselors would absolutely not be okay with any of them being up this late, and all he could think was how much he adored every one of them. It was fun.

And, now it was all ready. Everything as prepared as it was going to be. The whole thing was still bound to be a bit of a mess. But he thought it would be a good mess. Something that everyone really enjoyed. Maybe next year it would be a bit more organized.

The only thing left to get ready was himself. He applied his eye shadow carefully with a practiced hand, blending the colors together. It was bright and sparkly and had been a birthday present from his uncle. He was glad he'd packed it just in case without any clear idea of when he might use it. This was definitely an occasion worth doing his make-up for.

Taylor had gotten Mateo's advice on his outfit. He'd been video-calling Mateo for outfit advice since at least third grade. Taylor certainly did not trust himself with it. He liked wearing fun clothes for special events, but it was always hard to decide what went best together.

Luckily, Mateo loved that sort of thing. Taylor dutifully tried on outfit after outfit at Mateo's suggestion, until it felt like they'd used all of the possible combinations. Taylor advocated fiercely for his favorite shirt, and finally, Mateo agreed, although dubiously.

They had been able to coordinate with Coach Rose and the university to take over one of the larger classrooms for the show, and a smaller one next door to get performers prepped. That's where they found Wil, Jessie, Shonda, Alyx, and some of the other kids and counselors who were performing. Everyone was practicing at once, making for a very chaotic backstage. Taylor paused at the door to get his bearings before Wil caught his eye and waved them over.

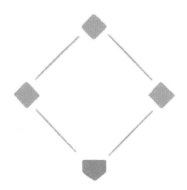

Wil

Wil had been fiddling with the music player when Taylor arrived, confirming over and over again that the music was queued up properly. He was just starting it again when a flash of color caught his eye and he turned to see Taylor and Mateo in the doorway.

Where Mateo was dressed simply in a solid blue button-down and slacks, and classy suspenders, Taylor was a burst of color. He wore tall rainbow socks and a striped rainbow skirt, along with some kind of patterned button-down. It wasn't anything like Wil's style but he looked great.

They came over and Mateo shuffled through some note cards while Wil explained the music player to Taylor. They chatted and watched some of the other acts get ready until Coach Rose arrived to let them know the show was starting.

The performers all filed into the larger room to watch as each act was called up in turn. The show was opened by a very chaotic group performance by the camp staff that involved a combination of dancing, miming, and singing, while Alyx juggled in the background.

The kids laughed and pointed out their favorite counselors to their friends, and everyone applauded when the whole group struck a variety of mismatched poses at the end. One by one, performers came up to show off what they could do. There were a bunch of singers, including a couple of pairs, and Shonda, who was on Wil and Taylor's team, did some ballet.

When Mateo came up to the mic, the room was silent. Wil leaned over to Taylor, "Does he sing?"

Taylor shrugged. "I dunno. He's refused to tell me anything. Stubborn like that."

No music started, and it was quiet for a few seconds until Mateo cleared his throat and said, "What do you get if you cross a tree with a baseball player?"

Almost immediately, Jessie stood up and shouted, "I dunno, what do you get if you cross a tree with a baseball player?"

"Babe Root!"

Wil immediately cracked up laughing while Taylor groaned next to him.

"What? You don't think it's funny?" Wil asked quietly, smiling.
"I think it's fine," Taylor whispered. "I've just heard all of his jokes a million times."

"Okay, okay, okay," Mateo continued. "I know you all know a little bit about baseball. But do you know how to win a baseball game without throwing a single ball?" A few people shook their heads. Wil heard Taylor sigh. "It's easy. See, you only throw strikes!"

Taylor

Taylor had indeed heard all of these jokes before, but he loved seeing Mateo tell them. He always lit up with happiness when he got someone to laugh and cracked up himself half the time. He had a great smile. He hadn't necessarily expected Mateo to actually do stand-up, but he was glad he did.

Taylor rolled his eyes through a few more well-worn jokes before he saw Colin waving at them from the outside aisle. "Hey Wil, I think we're up next." The two of them got up and carefully maneuvered to the side of the stage to get ready for their performance.

While Colin got their music queued up, Taylor adjusted his outfit. He noted Wil next to him, shifting restlessly. "You okay?"

"I'm just nervous. I always get a little bit of stage fright before performances. I don't think I need anything." Wil smiled and shrugged at Taylor, who couldn't quite read his expression but took Wil's word for it that he was okay. "You sure you want to do this?" Wil asked Taylor.

"Just because I'm a bad singer? Heck yeah, It's going to be fun. Unless... you don't want to?"

"I do, I just want to check in." Taylor took his hand and squeezed it.

"Okay. Let's go then."

Their song started and Wil and Taylor walked on stage together, Wil a few paces ahead. That was honestly really helpful because they'd decided to clap along to the beginning of the song and Taylor was awful at following the beat. Instead, he mostly watched Wil's hands and tried to match his movements. He had limited success, but he knew that would happen.

He bopped along to the song, enjoying it. "Centerfield" had been one of his favorites since he was nine and discovered that "baseball music" was a genre that existed. He had even talked his Nanay into performing it in a drag show with him when he was twelve, which was fantastic. They had borrowed a hat and jacket from his coach and he'd gotten his Ma to help him bedazzle an old Little League uniform. He still pulled up the video to show to every new team he was on.

He and Wil had spent a while going back and forth to decide what song to perform. But once Taylor suggested "Centerfield" and pulled up the old drag show footage, they'd both been convinced.

Then again, when he'd done it then, he got to lip-sync.

Wil burst out with the first verse, belting it confidently. He was so obviously in his element. Smack in the middle of their little stage area, arms spread wide, voice absolutely gorgeous. Wil clearly loved singing, but he was also fantastic at it.

Taylor had heard him sing before of course. Lots of shared evenings dancing around to music in their dorm room and a couple of rehearsals for the performance tonight, but nothing quite like this, with Wil singing full volume and really throwing himself into the song.

Taylor took the next verse, doing his best, but suddenly self-conscious of the obvious difference between his voice and Wil's. He loved singing too, but he seriously wasn't any good at it. That mostly didn't bother him. It hadn't bothered him until now. He'd been looking forward to this.

It was different actually on stage singing opposite someone as talented as Wil was, though. He finished his verse, grabbing a quick breath and reminding himself why he was doing this in the first place before throwing himself into the chorus with as much gusto as he could muster, both of them singing together.

Wil

"Oh put me in coach, I'm ready to play today
Put me in coach, I'm ready to play today
Look at me, I can be centerfield"

Wil hadn't ever heard the song prior to Taylor playing it for him. But it was perfect for this. Obviously, anything about baseball was a good fit for the crowd here. And it was light and high energy, made for a fun number.

Wow. He hadn't realized just how much he missed performing. It felt good to be doing something that he was actually good at. Something he knew he could rock. And it was just plain fun. Getting to share it with Taylor was extra special.

He looked so cute. His skirt clashed terribly with the slightly garish but still adorable baseball button-down he was sporting. But his make-up was perfect and the whole look was just so Taylor, for all that Wil wouldn't have been able to imagine it a week ago.

Wil was so gay for him. He had to fight to keep his eyes towards the audience and not let himself just stare at Taylor.

Luckily, performing came naturally. They'd practiced the song enough times that Wil didn't have to think about getting the words right. He could just throw himself into the moment and have fun.

When they finally finished, holding hands and throwing their arms up into the air dramatically, the amount of applause they received was definitely satisfying. It felt great to know that everyone enjoyed it. That he could do things that made people get out of their seats and clap. He'd always loved that part of performing.

Wil found himself hugging Taylor before they even made it off the stage. He just couldn't wait. "That was a blast," he whispered, still excited and riding the joy of performing. "Thanks for doing it with me."

"I had fun," Taylor said with an absolutely precious little smile, single dimple cute as ever, before taking Wil's hand and tugging him off the stage.

They wove their way back through the rows of seats to plop down next to Mateo and watch the rest of the performances. Mateo gave both of them a big grin and a thumbs up when they sat down, making Wil smile all the more.
At that moment, fresh off the excitement of a good performance, he wasn't even worried about the game tomorrow.

Of course, that changed quickly. By that evening he was a ball of nerves and Taylor had all of his usual pre-game antsiness, D20 flying fast as ever between his fingers. They tried to distract themselves with music with limited success. Wil didn't think either of them got a solid night's rest.

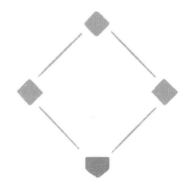

Taylor

Stepping up to the mound for the last game with a team always felt different. Top of the sixth, down one, Safaa at-bat. Taylor rubbed his die, took a breath, and wound up for the first pitch.

He loved the rhythm of pitching. He always felt safe and in control on the mound. He was the one initiating each play. And he was good at it. He knew most of these batters well enough to know what to throw them.

He made it through the sixth without allowing any hits.

"Nice." Jesed smiled at him when they headed back to the dugout.

"Hey, you're the one who set it up." Taylor grinned in return. Coming on as a closer could be stressful, but he rarely fretted when he played with Jesed. At least, he didn't fret more than he always did. She was a talented pitcher.
Both kids leaned up against the front of the dugout to watch the bottom of the inning.

It got off to a slow start, but Jordan scored a run toward the end of the inning, tying it up.

Seventh inning. If he could just keep it even, all his team needed was one more run and they could all head to lunch. Which would be ideal; he was hungry by now.

A couple of hits got through this time, but their basemen had it handled. No one made it home. And Wil caught Mateo stealing, which was absolutely fantastic. Taylor was so proud.

Mateo would definitely be pouting about that later that day. He'd doubled, which yeah kind of hurt Taylor's pride. Mateo genuinely was a great hitter though. And one of their outfielders had fumbled the ball.

But Mateo had never had any patience. He always tried to steal. Which, fair, it wasn't a bad strategy. But as long as they were playing against one another, Taylor was going to be happy he got caught.

Mostly though, he was just so impressed with Wil. He'd done perfectly, watched Mateo start to edge too far from base, and noticed the moment he got ready to run. He signaled Taylor and they had the ball to third in an instant. Mateo was tagged out a moment later.

"Way to go." Taylor pulled Wil into a big bear hug the moment he was off the field. "You did amazing! Too bad, so sad." He shouted over at Mateo with a friendly grin. Mateo stuck his tongue at him and Wil both.

Wil

Wow. He still couldn't quite believe he'd managed it. But he was in Taylor's arms and the inning was over and they were still tied.

Yeah, he hadn't done most of that, but he'd done something and that felt so awesome. Just like pulling off a complex dance number and knowing that he'd been part of bringing it together. Wil had watched carefully this time, but he'd also just trusted himself. Tried to at least. Worked on breathing and watching and using all of his strategies to stay grounded in the moment instead of worrying about making the wrong call.

It had worked. It was kind of amazing what a difference that one little thing made too. He'd already been way more relaxed coming into this game. The variety show actually helped a lot. Seeing his fellow campers be every bit as ridiculous as the theater kids he loved definitely made him feel a bit more comfortable with them, even the ones he still barely knew.

Plus, seeing Taylor, the terrible singer that he was, get up there and give it his all anyway somehow made him less worried about failing. The funny thing about anxiety was the more anxious Wil was about doing poorly, the more likely it was that he would.

Now he wasn't as anxious, he actually felt decently okay about batting, even with the score tied and everyone else seeming tense.

He could do this, kind of. And if he didn't, no one was going to be upset with him. It would be okay.

His at-bat came towards the end of the inning. They were still tied and it was hard not to start to stress. He was beginning to be anxious, but he tried to check in with himself and think about what he needed.

"Hey, Taylor," he asked. "Any chance I could have a reminder it's okay if I mess up or miss or whatever?" His cheeks were a bit hot, but otherwise, he felt okay. He trusted Taylor. Wil knew he wouldn't think that the request was silly.

"Of course. Wil, just do your best. It'll be totally okay no matter what happens. I'm gonna be proud of you no matter what," Taylor said, and now Wil's cheeks were even more flushed, but for totally different reasons.

Taylor spread his arms wide offering a hug and Wil accepted it gratefully before jogging over and grabbing a bat.
The first throw he judged it wrong and didn't swing when he should have. The second he swung too soon and missed. Wil tried to replay Taylor's words in his head. It was fine. He just needed to do his best. The third pitch came.

Crack!

He could hear the ball connect with his bat. The force of it always slightly startled him, but he'd learned how to stay on his feet. The ball didn't go far, and at first he thought it was going to be a foul, but given the crowd behind him yelling at him to run it must not be.

He dropped the bat and ran as fast as he could, somehow ending up on first, panting and absolutely exhilarated.

He was still catching his breath when he realized that the cheering hadn't stopped and the first baseman was walking off the field.

Oh. Shonda had made it home. He had kind of forgotten she was on third. Just in case you needed more evidence that this really wasn't his game.

They won! He batted in the winning run. The game was over just like that.

He jogged towards home plate and immediately got swept into a sea of hugs.

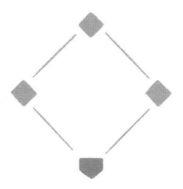

Taylor

That hit. Wow.

"That was amazing!" Taylor shouted over the celebratory crowd. He'd need to get out soon. It was already getting loud and overwhelming for him. But right now he was still reeling from their win.

Wil had perfectly bunted the ball. He doubted it was intentional. Wil had gotten better, but not that much better that quickly. Still, he'd swung at just the right moment and connected beautifully. And that was the game.

Walk off win in the bottom of the ninth with family in the stands. Hard to beat that. Especially after losing their last game.

Taylor hugged Wil long and hard before he made his escape, checking in first to remind him that he needed a bit of a break and to preemptively reassure him that it wasn't anything Wil had done wrong.

He'd seen how his post-game sensory overload impacted Wil before when he hadn't understood what was going on. And Taylor had a general idea that anxiety could twist anything into a negative.

Eventually, he was grounded enough to manage lunch in the dining hall with the whole group. Their parents and Jessie's aunt were here now. Mateo's dads had dropped the two off at camp, so Jessie's aunt was picking them up. Grand Junction really was obnoxiously far away.

Taylor knew that Mateo would be a bit sad his dads had missed the game. The two families swapped pick-up and drop-off duty every year so they took turns seeing the final games.

"Well played. That was a tight game," he said as he pulled Mateo into a full hug, dragging him up out of his chair.

"We almost had you," Mateo said with a grin, perking up a bit.

The meal was nice. Everyone was chatty and comfortable with one another, talking naturally even though some folks barely knew one another.

Sitting in the stands for the second game, one hand linked with Wil's and his other arm swung about Mateo just felt so good. He loved watching baseball with people who really got it. And having the rest of his family here with him just made it all the more special.

Jessie's team won in extra innings. And he was so proud.

By the time they were back in their dorm room, collecting the bags and mismatched luggage they'd all dropped in a conference room that morning, it was just beginning to catch up with him that it was truly the end of camp.
It was always easy to push it away on the final day. To let himself hyperfocus on the games, to enjoy seeing his moms again.

But once that second game was over, the reality set in hard.

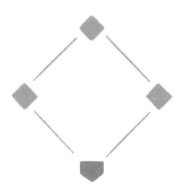

Wil

Three weeks ago Wil never would have imagined it would be this hard to leave. He tried to remember how he'd felt when he got here.

So anxious and unsure of himself. So positive that he'd never fit in. It hadn't been that long, but so much had changed.

He guessed he'd made a lot of assumptions. He'd had such a fixed idea of what sports camp would be like, what jocks were like. But it turned out they were just kids. Every bit as ridiculous and varied as anyone Wil went to theater camp with.

Mateo was sweet and super into fashion. Jessie was a delight and had way too much energy to be reasonable. The other kids he'd met were all friendly enough. Shonda was even every bit as much a theater person as he was, though apparently more into dancing than singing.

And Taylor. Taylor was kind and adorable and such an absolute geek about baseball and so wonderfully himself. Wil loved him.

At first, he'd thought that Taylor had everything figured out. He'd seemed so confident. Learned all kinds of formal vocabulary and theories from his professor Nanay and just was so open about himself and who he was.

On reflection, that was part of where things had gotten weird between them. He'd forgotten to let Taylor be human. He wasn't perfect at everything. That was wonderful too. Wil was growing fond of the awkwardness and carefulness and uncertainty that he was just beginning to recognize in Taylor.

Goodness, he was going to miss him.

"Can we stay in touch?" Wil asked, suddenly so anxious. He knew logically that they would. Taylor had even let Wil set him up a TikTok account so he could follow Wil. Reassurance from Taylor would help his anxiety settle down though.

"Of course," Taylor said readily, completely unfazed by Wil asking such a seemingly silly question. He always was. Wil loved that about him.

"And I'm gonna come to all your shows. So, you need to let me know when to get tickets. And you can come to my games if you want to. I even promise not to be bothered if you're on TikTok the whole time. You and my Nanay can look at it together."

"Your Nanay has TikTok?" Wil asked with a laugh. Having met them, he was absolutely not surprised.

"Yep. They use it for drag stuff mostly."

"Why didn't you tell me that? I have to follow them."

He felt more comfortable now. That was all he'd needed at that moment. Just the reassurance that Taylor still wanted to be friends, that he wasn't just going to disappear as soon as they got home.

"I'd love to come to some of your games. My dad will be delighted that I actually want to go to a sports game." It would be fun to go with him and at least be able to follow. Wil was glad that was something he'd be able to properly share with his dad now.

"We need to just hang out too. Slumber parties and all that." Taylor said with a grin and Wil got a sudden flash of Taylor in PJs with a face mask and bright nail polish, the classic sleepover attire. It sounded perfect.

Taylor

It was nice to have a friend from camp who lived close enough to realistically be able to hang out more than a few times a year. On rare occasions, he managed to get together with Jessie and Mateo for one of their birthdays, but that was about it.

Chatting with Wil, it was fun to realize all of the things they'd be able to do together. They didn't live super close, but it wasn't terribly far either. Taylor could probably bus to Wil's area in about forty-five minutes.

Taylor's moms hadn't always been big fans of Taylor taking the bus by himself, which definitely bugged him more and more as he got older. He was realizing now that he ought to actually talk to them about it though.

Both of them had been pretty chill when he asked them to stop messing with his hair. He shouldn't just assume that because he couldn't take the bus when he was ten, he still couldn't.

It felt weird to realize that he could bring things up. As a kid, he'd always just gone with the flow. But, he was older now. He could have those conversations with them.

He also probably ought to try his D&D baseball explanation on them. He'd spent the past several years basically repeating the same explanations indefinitely and hoping that eventually, they'd stick. Which to be fair, Ma had pretty much given up, but Nanay hadn't. He was glad that at least now he had an explanation that might work better for them. If it didn't, he'd keep trying. Maybe Wil could help.

"I'm gonna miss you," he said, crying and pulling Wil into probably the third or fourth hug in as many minutes. "We have to make plans soon. Before school starts, okay?"

Wil nodded his agreement. "Definitely. I'll text you once I'm home," he promised.

"I'm going to miss you all. It's no fair you two live so far away." Taylor turned to Jessie and Mateo.

"Hey, you're the one who lives far from us," Jessie tossed back, but she was crying too. It really was awful not getting to see each other all year.

"Yeah, yeah. Talk to my moms about that," he returned, wiping his eyes and hugging them both before they headed out with Jessie's aunt. It would be close to midnight before they got home, so they didn't have forever for long goodbyes.

Not that he and Wil necessarily did either. It was dinnertime already and standing here crying wouldn't change anything.

"Guess we ought to head out too." He glanced towards his moms for confirmation. Ma nodded, though she looked sympathetic. She'd been living with both him and Nanay too long to not understand how hard goodbyes were for them.

Transitions were awful. Taylor hated them.

"I love you," he told Wil, pulling him into his arms one last time.

"Love you too," Wil returned, blinking back his own tears. He wasn't as uncomfortable with them as he had been before though. Instead of trying to brush them away, he leaned into Taylor's soft sturdy frame, content to just be.

"Talk to you soon," he promised as they pulled away from one another. Shouldering one bag and grabbing another, he happily accepted his dad's help with the rest. He definitely packed too much.

Taylor's family was weighed down with even more stuff though. The last couple boxes of variety show costumes rested on Taylor's Nanay's hips while Taylor and his Ma wrangled the luggage.

They all walked out together, crowding into an elevator and making their way out to the parking lot.

"I'll miss you." Wil stretched up on tiptoes and waited for Taylor to bend down so he could kiss his cheek. Taylor squeezed his hand in return. Then, got into the car with his moms and drove away.

Wil was glad that his dad let them just stand and watch for a minute. They were some of the only people not moving in the busy parking lot. It seemed that getting everyone home at the end of the camp was every bit as chaotic as arriving had been.

Dad stepped next to him and put an arm around his shoulders, and the weight of it was heavy and comforting. "Have a good time at camp, son?" he asked, voice warm and loving.

"I actually really did," Wil said with a chuckle. "I didn't expect to. But I did."

His dad squeezed him once, then let go and made his way

toward their car. "I'm glad." He sounded relieved. "I'm sorry. I shouldn't have assumed you would want this. I just wanted you to know how much I support you. Plus, I guess I hoped that maybe baseball was something we could share." He sounded almost bashful again. Wil still wasn't entirely used to hearing his dad sound like this, but it was nice.

"It's okay," he reassured, joining his dad in the car. "Yeah. I don't think I ever wanna come back. But it was all right. I know you meant well. Just maybe next time we can actually talk about it instead of assuming?"

Dad nodded. "Absolutely."

"I will say, I'm glad I understand baseball better now. Sorry I never asked about it. You've always supported me with theater." Wil continued, feeling like that was important to name as well.

"I love watching you on the stage, kiddo. You come alive out there. Though it sure was fun seeing you bunt that ball too." He laughed.

"Is that what that's called? I swear I thought it was a foul for a moment."

With that, they were both laughing. Side by side, pulling out of the parking lot. Somehow, it was the most comfortable Wil had been with his dad in a long time.

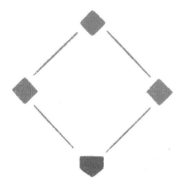